WHITE STAINS

WHITE STAINS

BY

ANAIS NIN & FRIENDS

Delectus Books
London 1995

First published c.1940

This facsimile edition published by Delectus Books,
London, England

Copyright © Delectus Books 1995
Preface © Michael R. Goss 1995
Introduction © C.J. Scheiner 1995

Delectus Books
27 Old Gloucester Street
London WC1N 3XX

ISBN: 1 897767 11 0

Jacket design & additional typesetting
by *image engineering*, 0181 968 6633

Printed by Woolnough Ltd.,
Irthlingborough, Northhamptonshire

CONTENTS

PREFACE

Before Cliff Scheiner's excellent introduction I would like to give a short account of the provenance of our copy of *White Stains*.

In 1989, Britain's premiere publisher of erotica during the 1960s and 70s died after a long illness. Charles Skilton, owner of Arthur Balfour's[1] mansion, just outside Edinburgh, had published more than a hundred titles under his famous Luxor Press imprint. The books, distinctive in their bright yellow covers were all published 1963-1975, many were reprints of erotic classics, some were ground breaking studies in sexology others were, er... shall we say, far less literary.

Skilton, who began his publishing career with Frank Richard's first Billy Bunter novels, was also one of world's few major collectors of rare and antiquarian erotica. I never met Charles, although we did share many mutual friends and contacts; it was through one of these that we bought the majority of his backlist before it went to auction. However most of the rarer books from his own collection were auctioned off at the house, with the remainder being auctioned at Philips in Edinburgh. Delectus had to battle it out to buy the best lots.

We came away very satisfied with our haul; that, I thought, was that. Then, late last year, I had a phone call from the buyer of Skilton's former residence informing me that they had found another cache of Skilton's collection in a basement storeroom that had been missed by the auctioneers. Within days, and with great anticipation, we were heading up to Scotland in a hired van. On arrival we were shown into a huge room shelved all around and full of books, and told to help ourselves. After removing what we wanted and stacking them on the floor we were shown to a smaller room and then I saw it, nestling, rather appropriately, amongst a collection of books on Paris. The spine of a book caught my eye, *White Stains*, immediately I thought it was the book of decadent poetry by occultist Aleister Crowley, an exceptionally

---

[1]British Prime Minister 1902-1905

i

rare book published by Leonard Smithers, the majority of the one hundred copies having been destroyed by H.M. Customs in 1924. I slid the book into the our growing pile without showing my obvious delight.

On the way back we decided to spend the night in Berwick-upon-Tweed and drive the rest of the way to London the next day. I took the copy of *White Stains* up to the hotel room to read only to discover that it was not the Crowley book, as I had first thought, but a book of rather excellent erotic short stories. I felt that it had some potential as a future publishing project, and that I had discovered something special, however I left it to one side while working on other titles.

Some months later I was visiting friends in New York, including Cliff Scheiner who told me, over a fine mexican lunch in Greenwich Village, the whole fascinating story of the book's first publication and that he had originally sold Skilton, some years before, the same copy of *White Stains* that we had bought last year. I immediately commissioned him to provide the introduction you are soon to read. I had always been interested in the Anais Nin/Henry Miller axis, in fact the two films made about Anais Nin and her circle always moved me to tears, *The Moderns* (1988 Dir: Alan Rudolph), and, more recently, *Henry & June* (1990 Dir: Philip Kaufman). In these films we see a generation in the midst of life, laughing, drinking, fighting, crying, their creativity in full flow. Several small, yet poignant paragraphs on the end credits to *Henry & June* informed us that it was Anais Nin's wish that the story could only be told after the last of the participants, Hugo, had died. Previous images from the film, its vibrant characters and with their voracious appetite for life and experience were played back by my memory. I realised these shooting stars had long since burnt out, suddenly I felt fragile, mortal, I cried.

Michael R. Goss
London 1995

INTRODUCTION

About the year 1940 there appeared one of the strangest volumes of *sub rosa* erotic literature to ever appear in the United States of America. What set it so apart from the vast majority of that day's erotica was that its fiction was extremely sensual, almost poetically so, and was more skillfully written than most of the literature of any genre of the time. The book also had a pronounced air of mystery. Literally every piece of information on its title page, *including its title,* was false or misleading!

The book in question was entitled: "*White Stains* by Ernest Dowson .... Privately Published by Isidor Liseux. Paris". The deceit was instantly obvious. The book was known to have first appeared in New York City at a time when Liseux was already nearly fifty years dead. The title page called for "Five Illustrations by *Aubrey Beardsley* In His Most Erotic Vein", but no illustrations of any sort, by anyone, were present. Those in the literary know immediately recognized the writing to be not at all in the manner of the famous fin-de siecle English poet and translator Ernest Dowson (perhaps best known in the United States for his works published by the London based Leonard Smithers, and for his work with Aubrey Beardsley's circle on such projects as the Smithers's published *Yellow Book* and *Savoy* magazines). Perhaps, some conjured, the author could be a different person of the same name?

But even the book's title rang false. There already existed an infamous, obscene, and sacrilegious tome entitled *White Stains*. It was no secret that that book (anonymously published by Leonard Smithers!) was the work of the English mystic occultist Aleister Crowley, and that that book had been banned, seized, and destroyed all over the world. Crowley's volume, *White Stains*, while erotic in a vein, for the most part disgusted those who read it.

The *White Stains* that appeared c.1940 was nothing like this. It was a somewhat schizophrenic production, being two disparate items in one. It contained, (as the second part, an explicit sex manual "The Contemporary (and most exhaustive) Love's Cyclopaedia"), which was preceeded by six unrelated erotic short stories, novellas actually, each

WHITE STAINS

By ERNEST DOWSON

Containing also the Contemporary (and
most exhaustive) Love's Cyclopaedia

and

Five Illustrations by
AUBREY BEARDSLEY
In His Most Erotic Vein

Privately Published by
ISIDOR LISEUX
Paris

The original title page reproduced from the Roth edition of White Stains.

one complete in itself. Where the "Cyclopaedia" was probably a rewriting of the 19th century sex instruction manual classic *The Horn Book*[1], presented in modern, direct, blunt, to the sexual point language, replete with socially unacceptable sexual slang, it was the fiction pieces that drew the attention and astonishment. The prose pieces were simple and lyrical expressions of complex erotic and sexual feelings. Sensuality rather than sexuality *per se* was the predominant theme, although the two were juxtaposed and finely attuned to each other. Even when graphic and sexually explicit, it was hard to classify these tales as obscene or pornographic. They were simply too beautifully written.

Over the years this c.1940 *White Stains* has yielded some of its secrets. The man responsible for its printing and publication in the United States has been reasonably identified as Samuel Roth, the New York City poet, author, book seller, magazine editor, publisher, mail order pioneer, and all around litterateur. (The printed book was even bound with Roth's signature red end papers as if a clue to the public). According to Gershon Legman, the dean of living eroto-bibliophiles and folklorists, Roth so liked the sound of the Crowley book's title he decided to reprint it sight unseen. However, when he actually read the book, he found it too vitriolic and scurrilous to dare put into print. Roth, ever resourceful, if not too much a spendthrift and unwilling to lose his invested purchase price of the Crowley tome, then opted to ignore the Crowley text, but keep the title for his own use! Roth simply appending to it a more agreeable erotic text. The attribution of this new book to Dowson may have been a typical Rothian marketing ploy, to attract the commercial attention of his literary mail-order book customers who were interested in the poet Dowson's crafted verse and prose. The title alone had already attracted the attention of those eager to obtain the infamous, tabooed, forbidden and almost never seen genuine Crowley item.

[1]Editors note: I examined the New Interesting Library edition of *Love's Encyclopaedia*, published sometime between about 1917 and 1935 (Mendes 206), in the British Library (P.C. 27.a.56) and found it to be virtually the same text as the *Love's Encylopaedia* contained within *White Stains* except that the typographical and punctuation errors have been corrected, and that the chapters in the *White Stains* version have been given additional subheadings not present in the NIL edition. Some words have also been changed, ass becomes arse and likewise strange (on P.31) has become queer in the later version (p.139) published as the second half of *White Stains*, however it is still evident that this manual has been derived from *The Horn Book*.

Who then wrote the six delicious novellas? That is no mean detective job. In form, style, and content they are very reminiscent of many of the Depression period commissioned ("dollar a page") erotica produced by Anais Nin and her many literary friends in New York. These *White Stains* short stories compare favorably with those acknowledged Nin pieces published openly for the first time in the late 1970s in collections entitled *Delta of Venus* and *Little Birds*. They are also in the same mold as the prose in a secretly produced 1950 typescript collection entitled *Auletris* by *"ANIN"*.

Understanding how these items of erotica came into existence sheds light on the possible authorship of the six stories in *White Stains*. During the American Depression jobs were at a premium, and many writers were unable to find any paying work in their field. One area of "literature" that still flourished, though, was pornography. Illegal, *sub rosa*, titularly suppressed, unless you had the right connections and made the right pay-offs, the fact was that any one who wanted erotica could get it with little problem. Mass produced sexually explicit eight page comic books, known as "Tijuana Bibles", or illustrated pamphlets of 16 or more pages, known as "readers", could be had for a dollar or less - not an inconsiderable sum in those days, hence the wide spread loaning and trading and reselling of these items among the common American populace. For more money one could buy full length novels that were mimeographed or rotogravured or actually printed and bound, as your budget allowed. At the acme of the heap, if you had the finances and the connections, you could purchase the cream of the day's pornography - the privately commissioned erotic story. With this prospect of large amounts of money to be made, in an otherwise economically depressed industry, "The Organization", as it came to be called, was created.

In the simplest terms, "The Organization" was a loosely connected group of booksellers and literary agents and authors in various American cities (especially in New York, Chicago, and Los Angeles). When trustworthy, "special" customers asked their booksellers if there was something "different" they could get, under the counter, the answer was "yes, for a price". Depression era writers, hungry for work or money or food, regularly asked agents, editors, and booksellers they were friends with for special projects. Those willing to deal in erotica decided that cooperation would be much more financially expeditious than direct competition with one an other, especially when they nearly all had already one element in common, a single main patron, the Ardmore, Oklahoma oil millionaire named Roy Melisander Johnson.

Roy Johnson claimed to own and have already read all the extant erotic texts which existed in English. Being unable to enjoy a second time any book he had previously read, he decided to commission new erotica for his private reading pleasure. He contacted the same people who in past years had supplied him with printed pornography and fine editions, mainly booksellers in large cities, and requested that they supply him with two new erotic books a week. As he was willing to pay $100 to $200 for each 100 page manuscript (more for anything from Henry Miller), the booksellers were happy to oblige.

Even though Johnson directed that half of his money should go to the authors, this was not always the case, and the authors for Johnson's erotica typescripts were frequently in the dark as to what their off-color literary products were really worth in the market place. Many of the booksellers were also publishers on the side, and because of the Depression, it was not hard for them to find out of work or struggling writers who were willing to churn out 100 page erotic typescripts for $1.00 a page, or much less, literally anything they offered. Equally, they could locate literary agents with other clients willing to join in this project, since money was short all over. The first authors recruited friends, and the ranks of those in the anonymous employ of the Oklahoma oil millionaire swelled. And so a new American cottage industry was begun.

The workings of "The Organization", while originally highly secret and clandestine, have recently been documented in various books published by former members of this erotica cartel. One need only read Anais Nin's *Diaries* (Vol. 3 especially), Bernie Wolfe's *Memoirs of a Not Altogether Shy Pornographer*, Milton Luboviski's affidavit published in "Henry Miller's" *Opus Pistorum*, or any of several Gershon Legman opuses, including his *Horn Book*, his introduction to Kearney's *Private Case*, or the yet to be published "On the Faking of Henry Miller" and *Peregrine Penis*. The authors for the most part worked alone, at home, at their typewriters. They turned in their finished manuscripts to the local agent, who frequently paid them less than the agreed upon $1.00 a page. Many found it increasingly difficult, if not totally boring, to produce pornography on a scheduled basis. To alleviate the tedium several of the authors in the New York area started to gather together, and formed a group which worked together for the common financial good, and the companionship it offered.

Anais Nin gives a wonderful description of how she and her friends (male and female) would jointly write erotic literature round-robin, (a technique employed decades later to produce such best-sellers as *Candy* by "Maxwell Kenton" and *Naked Came The Stranger* by "Penelope Ashe").

One can well conjecture what specifically Roy Johnson requested. Nin related in her diary how the unknown patron for her work once complained that he wanted less literary art and more lust in the stories he was buying! Nin further relates how the male homosexuals in her group wrote erotica as if they were women, while the "wall flowers" wrote about orgies, and the most sensitive and chaste of the group (after reading Krafft-Ebing's *Psychopathia Sexualis*) wrote of the most bestial perversions. Bernie Wolfe tells how he got kicked out of the enterprise for demanding more money, and then made a deal with Henry Miller, who at this time was no longer interested in writing pornography for the millionaire. These two agreed that Wolfe would continue to write pornography which Miller would then turn in as his own, with the two splitting the extra $1.00-$2.00 a page that the millionaire Johnson paid for erotica from "Henry Miller". (In an extremely technical sense Johnson got what he paid extra for, as these manuscripts did literally come to the New York agent *from the hand* of Henry Miller).

The fraternity of writers anonymously commissioned by Johnson was impressive. In addition to the above named, there were also Robert Sewall (the brilliant pastiche author of *The Devils Advocate*), Clement Wood (author, poet, editor, and bon vivant), Robert De Niro Sr. (poet and father of the famous actor), Robert Bragg (aka "Bob De Mexico"), Caresse Crosby (wealthy widow of the famous American expatriate publisher of Paris's Black Sun Press), Jack Hanley, Gene Fowler, Anton Gud, George Barker (the English poet), Virginia Admiral (the painter), Harvey Breit, Robert Duncan, Clifton Cuthbertson, Lupton Wilkinson Paul Little (the most prolific American author of erotica with over 400 novels to his credit), and many more whose names and deeds have over the years slid into literary obscurity.

Gershon Legman has written of how he gave over his part in "The Organization" enterprise (writing episodes for the very popular series of related stories known as the *Oxford Professor*) to his friend Robert Sewall as he (Legman) found that writing pornography made him impotent, a complaint later echoed by Henry Miller! When more episodes for the *Oxford Professor* were requested in short order, more writers were recruited to this project. Hence the series became a collection of related short erotic stories written by various authors over the period c.1937-1950, with the New York branch of The Organization providing the sequels to the original story.

How the individual stories became printed collections is of relevance to the creation of *White Stains*. Legman, Sewall, and the other commissioned erotica writers each contributed their chapters to their contact people, and received their pay. Realizing that more money could be made from these pre-paid stories through other venues, the agents and middlemen started having copies and carbon copies of the original typescripts made for their own hawking, e.g. carbons of the manuscripts were made and sold or rented to other customers.

The authors themselves soon caught on, and started keeping carbon copies of their works for their own use, as well. The ribbon copies of the text were sent to the millionaire, who probably never realized that his privately commissioned works were receiving a general circulation. Every so often, as the demand and opportunity arose, several of the stories would be published together by these enterprising entrepreneurs for their own additional profit, all unbeknownst to Johnson.

A representative, well known example of this type of publishing is that of the "Oxford Professor" series. The first of these collections was *An Oxford Thesis on Love*, first publicly published in 1938. Gershon Legman has identified Lupton Wilkinson, a Hollywood writer of British origin, as the author of the original *Oxford Thesis*. The eight separate pieces comprising that work seem to have been written on consignment for Roy Johnson, when the oil man first started to pay for new manuscripts for his reading pleasure. *An Oxford Thesis on Love* was followed the next year by the related *The Passionate Pedant*, which consisted of sequels to the former, written by New York area writers. Both of these books were crudely printed in mimeo form with erotic illustrations by the soon to be famous artist Emile Ganzo, founder of the "Woodstock School" of art. Other collections of these related stories subsequently appeared, in print, over the years under such titles as *Torrid Tales, South of the Border, The Professor's Tale*, and *The Oxford Professor*. This last title seems to have been published c.1950, octavo in size, poorly printed by offset, illustrated with copies of previously published erotic art and photographs, and badly perfect bound by a publisher who had bought several cartons of carbon copies of "The

Organization's" work from a former participant in its workings.

There was another method for the commissioned typescripts to get into general circulation, as documented by the dispersal of the erotic work that has come to be known as "Henry Miller's *Opus Pistorum*". As related in letters between the participants, copies of erotic stories written by the New York branch of "The Organization" were given to Henry Miller as he traveled across the United States in 1941, in the hopes that he could find publishers or booksellers along the way from New York to California who would pay to print or buy copies of the stories for their own customers. Miller met with some success, and additional stories were mailed to him en route. Thus the stories were promulgated, and Miller's name became indelibly connected with these stories, despite Miller's renunciation of them for many years.

What then are the answers to the questions posed by the c.1940 *White Stains*? In theory, one could imagine Sam Roth intercepting copies or carbons of typescripts meant for the Oklahoman, or commissioning some on his own (although that was not his style), or buying carbon copies from middlemen he knew in the publishing world, and surreptitiously printing them *sub rosa* to satisfy his dream for his own edition of a book entitled "*White Stains*".

The actual authorship of the delicate fiction in *White Stains* will probably forever remain speculative. The pieces in *White Stains* bring to mind again the complaint Nin noted in her diary for December, 1940, writing that the anonymous patron commissioning the original erotica she and her friends were authoring was unhappy because the pieces she and her friends were penning had too much *poetry*! This anonymous patron must have been the above identified Oklahoma oil millionaire Roy M. Johnson, who directed that he wanted stories that were narrative, direct, specific, concentrated on sex, and without philosophy or analysis. (Obviously Johnson did not appreciate that the mind, and not the groin, is the most erogenous part of the human body). Recent research on some of the most famous of the "dollar a page" erotica, the series which became the *Opus Pistorum*, attributed to Henry Miller, has attributed the authorship of these pieces in the main to Caresse Crosby, the friend of Anais Nin and Virginia Admiral, and the widow of the expatriate publisher, Harry Crosby, whose Black Sun Press in Paris was internationally famous in the 1920s and 1930s. Yet in the end, the extreme similarities of the stories in *White Stains* to those self-acknowledged stories by Nin – the language, syntax, perspective, cadence, etc., – can not be denied.

Over the years this volume has become nearly forgotten. No one has openly claimed it for their own, and only those fortunate enough to have found a copy of the increasingly rare original volume have had the opportunity to savor its pleasures and artistry, until this facsimile reproduction from Delectus.

C.J. Scheiner.
New York 1995

Alice

I USED to meet her at dances during the Winter. She was a wonderful dancer and a little beauty. Needless to say, holding her in my arms in dancing made me wish to know her better. It was not long before little pressures of hands and arms were asking, and answering unspoken questions. Without a word said, she let me know that some day she would consent to more.

Later, in the Spring, we used to go walking together in the hills on pleasant afternoons. We would drive out into the country, hide the car somewhere on a quiet road, and wander off into the fresh green woods. We were fond of a most secluded little glade which we found one day, where we often rested sure of being undisturbed. But Alice, though generous with kisses and dear little caresses, entirely withheld herself otherwise, and I was entiriely too fond of her, and too interested in discovering under what circumstances she would give herself, to press matters beyond

9

showing her clearly what I wanted. She quite understood, all the time, and I knew it was only a question of time until she would be brought to the point of giving me all that I asked.

Her surrender came under the unusual circumstances which I am about to describe. One lovely, warm afternoon in May we found our way to our little glade, but were very much surprised to find two other young lovers there before us. Totally engaged in each other, they did not hear us, and we stealthily withdrew a little distance and sat down in a little pocket among the bushes to see what would happen. Alice, I could easily see, was very much excited and interested.

The girl was lying on her back in the shade of a tree. The man lay beside her, and their lips were together. We could hear the indistinct murmur of their voices. Hunched up as we two were in our little hiding-place, quite close together, I did not find it hard, nor think it wrong, to put my lips to Alice's. Alice clearly thought my conduct fitting, for she returned my kiss, with interest. The interest was paid in a tiny flutter of her tongue-tip against my lips. Our kiss lasted quite a time.

When we looked again, the scene had changed somewhat. Alice gasped a little, and well she might. The lover was lying on one side, propped up on an elbow, and his free hand was disturbing the formerly smooth folds of his sweetheart's skirt. Perhaps to keep her attention from what his hand was doing—at any rate. to keep her attention divided—he was kissing her quite ardently. But his hand was under her skirt and had pulled it up so that we could see two shapely legs in pale blue stocklings. Two small feet in pale blue slippers (very unsuitable for walking in the hills) were calmly crossed. The lover was caressing the pale blue stockings.

"Peter," whispered Alice, remonstrating. For as she crouched, somewhat curled up, one very attractive leg, as far as the knee, lay outside of the shelter of her skirt, and my hand rested on the dark green silk that covered it. But her attention must have been distracted, for after that one remonstrance she leaned forward, her eyes intent on what she might see, while my hand enjoyed the delightful touch of green silk stretched over a beautifully modelled leg.

I turned from admiring the contours of the dark green leg to see what was happening to the pale blue ones. My hand, not being needed to see with, stayed where it was most comfortable. The blue legs had become most interesting. The skirt had been moved still more—the length of the blue stockings was now measurable. Not far above the knee they ended, and considerable was to be seen of two plump, white thighs, with the hand of the lover tenderly touching and stroking them. The pale blue slippers now lay side by side, and the girl's two arms, while her legs were being so lovingly caressed, were tight about the neck of her lover, holding his face to hers for kisses.

"Peter!" warned Alice again, in a tense whisper. For somehow, when I turned my eyes from the pretty green leg, my hand, left to its own resources without the guiding eye, had wandered somewhat; in fact, had strayed beyond the green stocking and was thrilling to the touch of soft, warm flesh. Alice stirred a bit, as if impatient, but it was satisfying to note that, in so doing, she thrust her legs still further from under her skirt. On looking to see what change her new attitude had effected, I was overjoyed to see that right close at hand there was a most enticing bit of plump, white thigh for me to appreciate. Close at hand, indeed; my hand made haste to embrace its opportunity, in fact to grasp at the unseen, as it felt its unhindered way to discover yet undiscovered pleasures to the touch.

12

"Pete, look-" whispered Alice again. And we looked. Not fifteen feet away the other pair, unsuspecting still, pursued their own amusement. The girl had moved—her skirt was drawn clear above her waist; her legs were all exposed, and her hips as well. Quite evidently the young lady had worn no panties or drawers! The young lover was sitting up, fussing with his clothing, his eyes enjoying a vision of loveliness. Those two pretty legs were slightly parted now, and such a dear little nest of hair was seen.

"Oh, Pete!"—Alice gasped this time. For, as the man's clothing was released, his sweetheart's hand reached out and took hold of something. The lover stretched out an instant, wriggled, and one bare manly leg came out of his trousers—bare, that is, except for shoe and sock and red garter. This bare leg was then placed across another bare leg, the man's between the woman's two, the woman's between the man's and satisfied with this arrangement the lover lay upon his sweetheart, his arms about her, hers about him. They moved delicately, as if rubbing on each other.

I had found Alice's hand and by placing it in a certain position I showed her that I, too, had something which might be held, should her hand care to hold it. Soon, indeed, she was holding it, and by playing with it as if absent-mindedly she caused me no little pleasure. But her eyes she could not remove from the scene before us.

We could hear soft cooings and murmurs. Alice and I ceased to regard the others for a time. She came somehow closer into my arms, lay quite heavily there, in fact, and is so placing herself managed to arrange her clothing so that both her legs lay bare. To my real surprise, Alice too was guiltless of drawers or panties. Much reassured, I let my hands move freely over the delicious surfaces of her thighs and hips. Our lips were fast together, and now I learned how Alice could kiss when really interested. When my hand in its wanderings encountered certain soft curls, her lips and her tongue assailed me with a quite impetuous ardor.

But curiosity drew my eyes again to the other lovers. "Look, Alice!" I whispered to her, and as we looked our hands became very busy and our eyes drank in a most lascivious sight. Side by side now the girl and her man were sitting, all outer clothing removed from their waists down, and the girl had further so opened her blouse that the dainty breasts hung out. With one arm each embraced the other, and their lips were crushed together. With their free hands they

14

were playing with the most delicious playthings that the hands of man and of woman can touch. The man's hand was moving between his sweetheart's parted legs, the girl's hand held something hard and stiff, which she manipulated gently.

"OO-oo-oh!" gasped Alice, and fell to kissing me wildly. Needless to say, I kissed wildly back. Her hand held something hard and stiff, and her treatment of it was as skillful as it was delicious. My hand was between her lovely legs, and the manner in which she received its ministrations showed that I had not forgotten how to play upon that organ which, if properly touched, causes a woman's body to re-echo with most delicious harmony.

Alice had at last abandoned her reserve, her withholding of herself. The discovery that she had worn no drawers gave me reason to suspect that this day she had intended from the start to give herself to me before our return. But, as a matter of fact, I had no knowledge based on proof of any kind that she ever had worn drawers, when, with me or at any time. As a rule, women wore drawers, or panties, or leg-covering of that general character—women in Alice's status in society, at any rate. This I knew from having seen them, from having removed them, in fact, on other and different occasions. It was not, therefore, an altogether unnatural assumption on my part that, under ordinary circumstances, Alice wore them also, and that she did not wear them this day because she had intended to be more than ordinarily gracious and complacent to me.

However, this is all a digression—Alice wore no drawers, and her very lovely naked thighs lay exposed to my hands and eyes. But her intentions towards me were shown even more clearly now by her conduct. Somehow, at some time, Alice had had experience. She had learned how to be charmingly wanton without being shameless. Her kisses were delights of art and skill, her movements were delicate and yet effective, her grip on what her fair hand held was possessive without being painful, and her handling of it, without being obtrusive, was obviously intended ultimately to bring it between her legs.

"Pete, darling, look there!" Alice whispered between her kisses. Our lovers were at last in earnest, the man lying between the girl's legs, which were embracing and holding him while he moved with vigorous thrusts of his hips. "Peter!" cooed Alice, and "Alice!" I cooed back—and somehow her weight was upon me, her legs spread far apart, and she took me into herself.

16

In the course of time we sat up again and looked about. The other pair were sitting up, smiling at us. We were discovered! In our excitement we had moved so that our former shelter
no longer concealed us. Strange to say, Alice did
not seem concerned. Either she was accustomed
to intimate acts of love with others—which I
really do not believe—or else she saw at once that
we must make the best of the situation and, perhaps, improve it. At any rate, she laughed quite
gaily and stood up, shaking her skirt down to
where it belonged. I stood up, too, but not so
easily, as my trousers needed attention.

The other man called out, "What luck?" "Fine,"
I said, "a bulls-eye!" Alice laughed again. "Same
here," he answered, stepping nearer, "my name's
Bill." "Mine's Pete." And we shook hands. I
presented Alice. She shook hands. "Gladys,"
said Bill, "here's Pete and Alice—come and get
acquainted." So, all introduced, we sat down,
Bill and Gladys on either side of me, and Alice
on the other side of Bill. We talked a bit, about
anything but the events of the past hour. But
after a time conversation waned. Bill was whispering to Alice, so I began to whisper to Gladys.
What I said was of no importance to the other
two, but it made Gladys laugh, with her eyes

shining. Furthermore, she put out her hand to see if what I had told her was true. Finding that it was, she seemed satisfied and lay back, smiling entiseingly. Somehow I found that I was embracing her naked legs. Bill did not seem to care—he was doing the same to Alice!

It was most interesting, to play this way with another man's sweetheart while the other man played with mine. There lay Alice, who had just given me a delicious half-hour, doing the same for Bill, and believe me I knew that Bill was lucky! And here lay Gladys, giving herself to my caresses as she had given herself to Bill not long before—and believe me, I soon knew that both Bill and I were lucky, twice!

Gladys was not so voluptuously formed as Alice, but she knew her part and made every little movement have just the meaning that it should. Her little breasts were just as satisfactory to my hands and lips as Alice's fuller ones, and she responded just as delightfully to the skillful touch of my fingers. She was all woman, and ended by giving me a most glorious moment as I scored another bullseye. Unless all familiar signs failed, Gladys received as much pleasure from my success as I did. Bill scored his second center shot almost at the same time. Both girls were flushed and radiant.

18

"Bill's bigger," confided Alice in a whisper as she nestled up against me, "but he hasn't your fiinesse, Peter darling. But it was wonderful to get that twice—oo-oo-oh!" Gladys was whispering to Bill, and I heard his heavier voice whisper back, "I'm glad you liked it, honey"—so I guessed that Gladys told him she had been pleased.

Bill produced some liquid refreshment. I don't drink much, but it was awfully good whiskey, and the little glass went around among the four of us several times. The girls got just a little drunk, and I began to get interested. There is something about taking a girl who is just a little bit intoxicated that is most fascinating. Even the ardent ones become just a bit more so, and the movements of a girl on the way to becoming drunk are most wanton.

It wasn't so very long before all of us, stimulated a bit, were huddled in a most intimate group. The girls lay all over us two men and kissed us with wet lips. We fondled them and kissed them, on the lips and on the nipples of their breasts, which they had left bare. The whiskey and these caresses soon had their effect. "Pete, what's that?" Alice exclaimed, and made her eyes round with mocking amazement. For there it was again, as large as ever! Gladys, see what I found, see

19

what I found!" Alice called, as she unfastened my trousers and held her discovery in her hand. Gladys without a word unbuttoned Bill, and took out what she found. No doubt about it, Bill's was bigger. But the girls were each satisfied— I know we all four laughed at the picture: two very pretty girls, somewhat flushed with whiskey, their breasts bare, each sitting beside a recumbent man and holding in her hand something she never could claim as her own except a man gave it to her. We all took another drink.

Alice was getting very gay, and her kisses more and more amorous. She handled me lovingly, and called me, or that part of me which her hand held, all sorts of amusing names. But I was surprised when, with a sudden change of position, she put her head down and began to kiss it. Gladys immediately did the same to Bill. We two men lay there awhile, too contented to speak, and watched our sweethearts kiss and suck us. Alice knew how to use her mouth! I have often wondered and have never found out, where and how she learned it.

Neither man nor woman could stand that for long. Gladys curled around and got her leg over Bill, and Alice imitated. I soon felt her, after a bit of rubbing, slide down upon me, hot and moist.

The girls rode us so, and rubbed upon us as we bounced them with our knees and hips. They laughed and exclaimed and crooned and cooed, each holding the other's hand as they jounced about side by side on their willing mounts, and they must have given each other some signal, for both sat erect at almost the same moment with that look of wondering delight that lovers love to see on their sweetheart's faces, and then collapsed together, gasping, as Bill and I rang up our third bulls-eyes!

It was now getting late. We all promised to meet again, and went our ways. On the road home lying with her head against my shoulder as I drove, Alice made the most extraordinary remark I ever heard from her lips—"Pete, I'm fucked to a frazzle!" Perhaps she was, then, but after a couple of cocktails and dinner at her house (friend husband being away) she invited me to her room, and there, on her own bed, and all naked this time, both of us, at her own request, I—well, the lady used the word first—fucked her again!

And as she lay there, stretched out so beautifully and happily naked, when I kissed her goodnight and good-bye, she murmured tenderly "Four times in one day, each time a wonder, but, Peter

darling, the last was the best!" And as I recall
her naked body in my arms, with every fibre leap-
ing with passionate desire, I still think it was the
best.

Esmeralda

HE WOMAN placed the lamp on an old table, descended into the stairway and closed the trap after her. As her footsteps creaked down the miserable stairs, Phoebus hastened to push the floor bolt in place. The old woman heard the sound, and laughed to herself, saying, "It's many a lesson master Phoebus will teach her before sunrise."

And now the officer was alone with the fair prize he had persuaded to come to this secluded garret with him. Well she knew, virgin though she was, the object of his desire. And now, as she found herself alone with him, in spite of her love for the handsome soldier she was blushing, trembling and confused, as he came from the fastening of the trap and seated himself on a great old chest beside her. Next to the chest, the foot close against it, was a dingy old bed.

For some moments he held her dainty hand in silence. Her cheeks were flushed; her long drooping lashes shaded her eyes. The officer, to whose

23

face she hesitated to raise her glance, was radiant. A luxurious warmth was already stealing through his eyes began to grow misty. At last, with trembling voice, she said, "Oh my lord Phoebus. Do not despise me. I feel that I am doing very wrong."

"Despise you, my pretty child," he replied, and why?"

"For coming here with you."

"On that point, my beauty, we are not agreed. I should not despise you, but hate you."

"Hate me!" she cried, in startled eagerness, "what have I done?"

"For requiring so much urging," she replied.

"Alas," said she, "that is because I am breaking a sacred vow. But what does that matter? Why should I need father or mother now?"

So saying, she fixed her large dark eyes upon the captain; she was silent for a moment, then a tear fell from her eyes, a sigh from her lips, and she said, "I love you."

There was such an odor of chastity, such a charm of virtue about the young girl that Phoebus had not felt entirely at his ease with her. But this speech emboldened him.

"You love me," he said rapturously, and he

24

threw his arm around her waist. He had only waited for such an opportunity.

"Phoebus," she said, gently removing his eager hands from her girdle, "I love your name; I love your sword. Draw your sword, Phoebus and let me see it."

He unsheathed his rapier with a smile. She studied the handle, the blade, examined the letters on the hilt with adorable curiosity, and kissed the sword, as she said, "You are a brave man's sword. I love my captain."

Phoebus took advantage of the situation to imprint on her lovely bent neck a kiss which made her start up red as a cherry.

"Phoebus," she resumed presently, "walk about a little, so that I may have a good look at you, and hear your spurs jingle. How handsome you are!"

He rose and gratified her; he walked about a little, gazing at the fair face and form of the beautiful creature; then he came and sat again beside her. Passion was now beginning to work in him.

"How hot and stuffy this old garret is," he said;" you are lighter clad than I and do not notice, but I am suffocating. This May night is like early Summer."

And, without comment from the girl, he arose and took off the heavy collar, belt, sword and outer garments which the custom of those times prescribed for an officer, and the heavy boots with the jingling spurs, leaving but his knee-length trousers and his long stockings to cover his limbs, while above his waist but a thin undergarment covered his body. Esmeralda started involuntarily as she saw his action, but again relapsed into thoughtfulness. Then he came and sat beside her again, this time very closely. The warmth of her body quickly penetrated the thin garment which he wore, and still further intoxicated him.

Words of love rose to his lips, to which the happy girl listened with increasing delight. Wrapped in her own thoughts, she dreamed for some moments to the sound of his voice. With arm around her waist, unhindered now, he pressed her and again told her of his love.

"Oh, how happy you will be, how happy you will be tonight!" he murmured at last, and gently undid her sash. This rude action startled her from her reverie for a moment, and then she again became pensive and silent. Made bold by her gentleness, he again lovingly presssed his arm around her waist, and then silently removed her

26

girdle. She was still dreaming, and with ardent gaze and trembling hand he began to unfasten her bodice. Hardly was this delightful task half performed when the soft garment began to fall away from the bright neckerchief which it had held in place. The blissful lover, quick to seize the opportunity, drew the pin which held the folds of the handkerchief together, raised her slightly from the wall against which she was leaning, and snatched it off. Her lovely shoulders, rosy and polished, shone above the top of her loosened bodice. She started like a frightened fawn, as she realized that his eager eyes were feasting on her nakedness, even so little, but almost as quickly she became dreamy again and let him have his way.

And the captain quickly applied his active fingers to the remaining laces of her bodice; in a moment the task was finished; it was entirely open, and through the filmly gauze of her chemisette he saw the lovely hillocks of her beautiful bosom. With a cry of joy, he slipped the bodice off first one arm, then the other, and madly tossed it away, while to the rapturous lover whose white arms seemed worthy of Venus herself.

Gasping for breath, he devoted his attention to her skirts, eagerly he loosed them. Then he knelt before her; removed her slippers. Boldly now placing his hands under her garments up to her knees he unfastened her stockings; he pulled them both off. She started involuntarily when his hands touched her limbs, but again became passive, though with an ever increasing flush on her cheeks.

Then he murmured to her to remain quiet, he rose quickly to his feet, and with mad eagerness tore off his remaining garments. In a trice he was naked, and study and white as Apollo himself, a splendid specimen of manly vigor.

Now he stood boldly before her, he cried out, "Esmeralda, be mine," and extended his hands. The dreaming girl was roused from her reverie by the sound of his voice; she opened her eyes wide, saw the ugly red bandage of his lusty manhood before her, and for an instant she hesitated and turned her head away, the last resistance of virgin modesty in the first presence of lusty manhood (not uncommon at such a moment). Then he spoke, with tones tenderly passionate; nature overcame that momentary hesitation; the inborn desire of the flesh asserted itself; she gazed into his eyes an instant, her own brimming with moisture; his hands were still stretched to her; and she rose to grasp them.

As she did so, her two loosened skirts fell to the floor, and the gauze of her chemisette, reaching only half way to her knees, was all that covered the trembling beauty. He took her hands, and she stepped out of those perfidious garments. Then for a brief instant he gazed into her sweet face; he saw in it the answer to his own glowing passion; then with hands shaking with excitement he undid the fastening of that last garment; it fell open at the neck; one last instant he stopped, before the final unveiling of those lovely beauties; then he pushed the straps off her shoulders; the garment was soft as silk and dropped unhindered to the floor.

His whole body trembled as he looked upon her naked flesh. Her hands and feet were most dainty; her arms and legs exquisitely turned; the rosy freshness of her skin heavenly. With all these, she possessed fullness of breast more voluptuous than classic, and hips of almost Eastern heaviness, withal, there was a suppleness and vigor in her appearance that told the practiced eye of Phoebus that here was the richest prize that he had yet been permitted to gather to his arms.

With an effort he restrained himself from seizing her, as she stood there with eyes half closed, but he laid his hands upon those polished shoulders, thrilling even at that touch of her fair skin, and exclaimed in a voice broken by passion, "Esmeralda, tell me again that you love me."

And she, gasping too, with emotion, cried out, "Oh come, do with me what you will; I am yours. Take me, take everything. What is my mother to me now? You are my mother, for I love you Phoebus, my adored captain, it is I; look at me, it is that little girl who comes in search of you. My soul, my life, my body, are yours. I am all yours, my captain. I will be your mistress, your pleasure, when you will; always yours. Take me, Phoebus, this is all yours."

As she said this in a voice choked with passion she hung her soft arms around the officer's neck; she gazed into his face imploringly, her beautiful eyes swimming with tears, and an indescribable smile on her lips. The enraptured captain, though careful not to allow his body to touch her, pressed his lips to those beautiful shoulders. The young girl, her eyes fixed on the ceiling, her head thrown back, trembled beneath his eager caress. Then finally he joined his burning lips to her own, and each drank in from the other a long draft of love. With moisture now falling over her eyelids, they kissed long and

30

deeply, till at last, in a little closer embrace he allowed her snowy hillocks to be pressed for the first time, though careful not to let his hips reach hers, nor his lustily throbbing tool to scarcely approach her snow white form. But that pressure of her luscious breasts was a charming introduction,for her, to the beautiful story which she read that night, the first true beginning of that sweet delight of the flesh, the first step in that delicious contact of strength and beauty which ends in the dizzy climax of the supreme inner kiss of Venus triumphant.

And when her breasts joined the thrill of their pleasure to the sweet sensation she was drinking in at her lips, the new delights were too much for the young girl, and she leaned heavily against her lover. He understood and led her to the old couch, whose dingy furnishings were now to be the bridal bed of Esmeralda, whose glorious beauty would lend to that old couch the charm of the King's own.

She lay down upon it, and moved toward the back, she knew he would soon be beside her. He stood, partly turned away, for a short time, gently caressing his inflexible rod of steel, burning to possess the treasure house of the lovely maiden. Then he came to the bedside, and looked down

31

upon her. With parched lips, distended nostrils, and swimming eyes he gazed for a brief moment upon the round, full titties, the richly developed thighs, the amply cushioned hips, and, in the midst of this rich whiteness, the mossy nest of dark hair which surrounded the place where were soon to be gratified their now mutual desires.

Her languor gave place to ardor. She opened her eyes, turned slightly toward him, caught his lustful gaze fixed upon her treasure house; for just one last instant, as she looked upon his rod for the last time before it ravished away her virginity, a slight feeling of dread came over her, then desire again conquered, she was willing, nay, anxious, now to know what were the sensations which this crimson instrument of torture could impart, and she stretched out her shining arms toward him, smiling.

Instantly he placed himself beside her, quickly placed one arm beneath her neck and shoulders, clasped the other around her warm body, and drew her full length against him. And she, too, threw her lovely arms around him, pressed her supple form close to his body, and then, each thrilled too greatly for words by that exquisite contact of the flesh, they lay a long time in silence, immovable, only the heaving of their breasts as they were pressed together, and the constant throbbing of his tool extended between his belly and her fair, white form being an exception to that loving rigidity.

Then, after what seemed an age of pleasure. and the inexperienced girl had been thrilled through and through by this embrace, he moved down just a little, placed one leg over hers, and allowed the heat of his tool to nestle in the mossy fringe a little above that love spot where their supreme love was soon to be consummated. It was too much for her equanamity; at that near approach of the male engine she cried out, and pressed her hot lips close against him. Firmly she held her body to that steel. Then he, teasingly, moved back a little, but now she pressed close to him as he did so, unwilling to lose any of that contact. Then they played many times thus; now the hairy, muscular leg of the man would embrace the white fairness of the girl's limbs, and, when he drew away, she would embrace his in turn. But each was careful not to separate far enough to take for very long that fiery spur from the mossy nest where its rod head was buried, only a couple of inches above the amorous lips, beyond which lay paradise, and directly under that mossy covering, already drink-

ing in, through the skin, the magnetism of that
lusty steel, was her exquisitely sensitive clitoris,
fully distended, and throbbing with mad anticipation. The girl was now sighing and moaning
with delight, and Phoebus was charmed immeas-
urably by the delightful beauty and her steady
and rapid advances toward the beginning of the
real act, which was now at hand.

For the heat of her hips, covered with perspir-
ation, the sexual odor which her whole body began to give out, the steady pressure of her firm,
round breasts against him the moisture which
filled her eyes and now and again overflowed on
her cheeks, told him that the time for taking full
possession of the beauty had come.

Gently he turned her back, still holding her
against him, though relaxing the pressure upon
her love spot as his weight came upon her, and
moving his rod backward, so that when he had
her entirely upon her back and lay full length
upon that sweet body his rod was poised between
the snowy luxuriance of her thighs. Quietly they
lay again for some time, until she became accustomed to the weight of a man upon her, and realized the fact that that very pressure, upon the
breasts of a girl who is not regularly thus treated,
is productive of a pleasant sensation.

Then at length, when he thought she was prepared for the great lesson, he gently raised himself slightly and with his right hand sought the love spot and carefully pushed away any hair which might have covered the treasure. Then he moved his lusty tool toward the entrance. With his right hand he pressed it down a little, till it was just at the gateway, he moved forward just a little more. It touched the moist lips, another slight movement, another; a smothered cry from the girl, and his head was inside.

The utmost care was necessary to keep from spending; she had almost overpowered him already by her intense magnetism; so he remained motionless a short time; both hands were now underneath her shoulders. Absolutely still they lay, though he could distinctly feel the mad beating of her heart. So they remained quiet, till he felt he was fully in control of himself, for he knew what she, in her innocence, did not understand, that a severe trial must come to both their passion could be realized. Her sacrifice of pain must be made before her fruits of pleasure could be gathered.

So now, being more calm, he gently began to push the tool into that virgin sheath. She could not remain quiet then, but gasped and moaned with every fresh movement. The distension of her sheath by that steel caused as continual an augmentation of her sensations which were those of delight only, until he had advanced about half the length of that rod when she suddenly drew back, involuntarily. He had reached her maidenhead. Now, for the first time, he had to reassure her, telling her that there would have to be a little pain before their pleasure could be consummated, but only for this once, and ever after that nothing but joy would attend the operation. With such words he calmed her as best he could, then clasped her soft shoulders, and made his first charge, a rather strong one, at the barrier. It held firm, but the girl cried out with pain. He knew it was useless to talk her any more, for the deed had to be done, regardless of the pain, before they could complete their divine union. Again he drew back slightly, and pushed against the membrane. It still held, and poor Esmeralda cried aloud. Another backing, another push of the tool, and another failure, but now the poor creature was frightened. "Oh, Phoebus, spare me," she moaned, "spare me. Oh, I'll do anything for you, but let me go. Oh, please let me go. Oh, oh, oh." He knew he could not, for it would have to be done some time if he released her, she would be too frightened some other time to undergo the ordeal. So he waited a little, and pleaded with her, cheered her as best he could, and tried to calm her fears, though not entirely successful.

But when she was somewhat quiet, he again, without speaking, braced himself for a fourth trial; his hot hands clasped her shoulders again, his feet were against the chest, he drew his horn back half an inch from the bar, and charged it again. Again no result, except a scream of pain from the panting girl; though her fair arms clung around him, she bitterly lamented her fate now. But he, in silence, drew back again; a fifth ram, and only cries and sobs. Oh, how he pitied the poor lamb; to whom he was forced to be so cruel. Tears stood in his own eyes, as he raised his head and looked into her dear face, drawn with pain, the lovely eyes dim with crying, and he sank down and poured his own tears upon her neck. But nature roused again. Again he drew back his thus far baffled tool; over half an inch away he stopped; gave another push; but oh, unhappy girl, only your sad cries were the result. "Oh, my darling Phoebus. I can't stand it. I can't stand it. I can't. I can't. Please, please, let me go. Oh, Phoebus; please; help me; Please! Please!! PLEASE!!!"

But he did not answer; he felt that the poor
girl's agony must be ended, at any price; he could
not endure those pitiful cries; there was but one
way, and that was the right way, cruel though
it might be. He put his hands quickly under her
shoulders harder than ever, he drew back over
an inch from the barrier, he braced his sturdy
legs hard against the chest, the unhappy girl
sobbed aloud as he did so; but he was adamant;
and this time his rod was adamant too, for he
gave a massive thrust, its hard head struck the
bar vigorously, and it broke and the impetus of
his stroke caused him to pass a good inch beyond
it, while the poor creature screamed aloud again
and again. Had one outside listened, he would
have thought the unhappy lass was being severely
punished, instead of being prepared for the consummation of the greatest happiness that could
come to her. Her pain, however, was most real,
and for a long time after the conquering of her
last resistance to her violation, she lay there and
sobbed and her dear body quivered with emotion.

But all things have an end, and eventually she
became calm. He encouraged her all he could,
and gradually nature began to instill passion into
her veins again. He moved slightly in that clasping sheath, and the healing oil with which he

had anointed his tool before possessing her had done its work, and the motion gave her only pleasure. The instant she realized that, her passion increased rapidly, and soon he felt emboldened to push on toward the goal. As he advanced further into her treasure house, the pressure upon her mount of venus became heavier; the exquisitely sensitive organ which lay beneath that mossy hillock was forcibly diminished in size, and every added pressure upon it added to her sensations of delight.

Now both were eager for the climax. The ever increasing heat of the beauty, only temporarily subdued, caused in Phoebus an irresistible desire to try the powers of the fine white body he embraced and to bestow upon the lovely virgin the first burning stream of passion from man's loins, while as for Esmeralda, now that the pain was over, she was not only sexually anxious, but mentally curious, to know the manner in which that rod would operate to end forever her state of maidenhood.

He took a firm hold beneath her soft shoulders, this time it was to give her the divinest of pleasure; she knew it, and wrapped her lovely arms tightly, one around his neck, the other just below his shoulders. An observer would have noted the ecstatic look on her face as he stiffened his arms, pressed his legs against the old chest, and pushed his rod of steel half an inch within that sheath. Then, for the first time, those maiden lips which guarded her supreme sanctuary felt the touch of a man; from head to foot the virgin trembled at that first kiss; she cried out with joy. For an instant, fearful of too sudden a result, he drew back slightly; then, when each had recovered from the first shock, he again placed the head against the sanctuary. And now, from the conjunction of those parts, a thrill of delightful sensation began to flow back and forth between them. Rising from her virgin lips, as they were pressed by that hot head, she could feel that thrill of exquisite pleasure rush up through her spine to her brain, most beautiful visions passing before her eyes; than plainly she could feel it descend again to her treasure house and flow in an electric current into his iron spur, and then she could feel him quiver slightly as it mounted to his brain and filled him with the glorious bliss it had her. Again and again it flowed back and forth from one to the other, and with each return to her body it was more intense, more delightful than before. More tightly she wrapped her arms about him; she pressed her fine legs close against him;

higher rose her pleasure; still more tightly she clung to him; quicker and quicker came her hot breath. He exerted every effort of will to prevent throwing the rush of his passion into her, as she panted and quivered and clasped him, and suddenly, as he expected, her arms and legs relaxed, the rigidity of her form was gone in an instant, she lay perfectly quiet. He raised his head; her eyes were half closed; her cheeks were crimson with passion; she was giving up the first tribute of her fountain of love; it was her virgin oil, this time, which never can flow but once, that was pouring from her cup to anoint the conquering instrument of the lucky Phoebus. Very quickly he felt its effect on the head of his tool; with difficulty he restrained himself; his breath came quicker; his hips began to twitch in spite of himself, so eager were the driving muscles to ram the beauty. Now his head was bathed in the steady flow, and every instant it sent a deeper burning thrill through his nerves. He could not last much longer, but now the girl was fast recovering her strength. He raised his head once more; she opened her eyes wide, they were brimming over again, but this time with the intoxication of her present and anticipated happiness. She wrapped her glorious arms around him once more;

she again pressed her ivory legs close against his. Her virgin tribute to her lover had been paid, and now she was eager to give up that virginity.

With a mad cry he tightened his arms, he stiffened his legs against the chest; he pushed the ravisher against the thrice willing victim firmly.

The sight of those two white bodies in that divine embrace was indescribable.

With every nerve and muscle tense, they strained their eager forms together.

There was one last supreme instant of silence, immobility, exalted anticipation.

Then a mighty THROB shook the whole length of that vigorous tool, nestling in her virgin lips.

She realized the climax was close at hand.

They gasped, once, for breath.

A second THROB, stronger than the first, the seed was near the goal.

The secret of life came to her.

For with the third magnificent convulsion, the FIRST STROKE OF THAT PASSION SEED was thrown upon her treasure house.

Her purity was gone forever. But the divine glories of heaven itself were hers.

She screamed aloud, as she felt that first destroying and revivifying blast of passion's substance, the happiest cry a man can hear, that of the despoiled virgin who is happy.

He had cried out, too; a sound strange to her; a girl hears it only once; it is the rejoicing in the delighted ravishment of a virgin eager to learn all that life has in store for her.

A second massive stroke dashed its hot fluid all over the deflowered place, and she again cried in ecstasy, but this time her cry was that of knowledge gained, and desire consummated.

Then as his lusty strokes continued, pouring their hot cream upon her she began to struggle with pleasure under its lashings. She cried aloud again and again:

"Oh, Phoebus, please let me go. Let me go. Let me go. You are killing me, Phoebus. Oh Phoebus, I love you, I love You, I love you so. Oh, Phoebus, please let me go. Please."

The lover had heard such words before, though surely never from as charming a creature as this. He began to bend his back slightly and move his horn forward and back. The motion was maddening to the already agonized girl. She cried out in supreme passion as he thus tortured her. He rammed a little harder; and again, sweet music to his ears, she moaned out:

"Oh, Phoebus, my love, let me go. Please!

43

Please! Oh, my love, my Phoebus, what are you doing, what are you doing to me? Don't kill me! Don't kill me. OH DON'T—DON'T—PLEASE, OH PLEASE—DON'T!!!"

She swooned away, as his attack ceased. Her defilement was complete.

Slowly they returned to earthly consciousness, gradually the fierce heat of their passion cooled. But for some time the fair bride of love clung closely to the man who had violated her chastity; then after many a whispered word of love was exchanged, and her happy sighs, he gently disengaged her fair arms, and carefully withdrew.

And as she law there her bosom was still heaving with the rush of her feelings. The beautiful round globes which had seemed so lusciously large when the flimsy chemisette fell from them were well pressed down from the attack they had experienced. Her eyes were still staring; her dishevelled hair lay round her shoulders; her fair, round arms lay quiet at her sides. In that short space of time, long as it has taken to tell it, she had been transformed. But her thoughts, when thoughts returned, were not of regret. The world had revealed itself to her in a new light, and she, though physically fatigued for the moment, was supremely happy. The modest, trembling confused virgin, who had entered that garret so short a time before had been touched by the magic wand of man's strength, and now she lay there holding in her treasure house, so ruthlessly violated, the invigorating seed of her lover's loins. Her maiden purity was gone, but she realized from that one blissful experience, the wealth of her own charms, and knew what they meant to a lover, and was not agrieved at the discovery.

After a time she rose from the bed for a few moments, and then, when she was ready, came in her sweet nakedness back to it, and lay down again. Well she knew that their night of love had only begun; that soon again her gallant lover would seek her fair body for their mutual delight.

Then Phoebus approached the bed, she turned first her shining dark eyes, then her lovely white body freely toward him, with very different feelings from those with which she had met him the first time. His strength had returned, for he was in full lusty health and vigor, and he gazed with sensual eye upon the loveliness of the girl he had so madly violated. And the appeal of those shining eyes, those warm lips, those lovely titties, those ivory legs, those sweet white arms, those ample hips, and that dark nest of love in the midst of that white voluptuousness, could not be resisted. He quickly lay down beside her, and they closely embraced again. Again and again he kissed her hot lips. This time it was a novice, but an ardent young beauty that he clasped in his arms; she had tasted the luscious fruit, foolishly called forbidden, and was soon eager to repeat the feast. Nature urged her on; the hot breath and lustful kisses of her lover roused her desire to draw from him again a tribute of his strength to her beauty. His animation was heightened by the increasing warmth of tne happy girl, who now lay panting on his greast, half on top of him, offering herself again to be loved. Again his organ pressed against her fair body. She felt its hot head against her Her animated curiosity, now no longer restrained by modesty, made her bold enough to slip her dainty hand down and grasp the lusty instrument which had violated her virginity. She wrapped her soft fingers around it and squeezed it gently, she ran her hot hand down to his hairy storehouse and grasped it in her warm clasp. Several times she pressed the hairy nuts in her unaccustomed hand, you must pardon her, fair reader, for she had never seen a man all for herself before, and her interest in his make-up was perfectly natural. She pressed, as I have said, the hairy balls in her dainty fin-

46

gers, the hot head of his throbbing rod lying along her soft, white arms as she did so. And with every pressure of the bag, drawn up tightly as it was, a thrill went through him from head to foot. She noted this, and laughed at his uneasiness. He was soon trembling with passion, and mad to mount her. Convulsively his hips began to work the tool up and down against her lovely arm, as he held her against her.

She knew what that movement meant now, and she would not have that treasure seed spilled, except just as nature intended it. She instantly let go his bag, took her hand away, clasped both arms around his neck, and crowded her luscious hips against his tool. Clinging together, she turned on her back. She cried with joy as the pressure came on her mons veneris. Once more his hand sought the love spot; with breathless eagerness she remained in absolute silence, while he pressed his head for the second time against her outer lips; eagerly they welcomed the steel spur now, not a stranger, nor a ravisher, this time, but a loving friend in the fair one's distress.

With delicious cries of happiness she received it as it entered her hot sheath, and advanced toward her sanctuary, unhindered now by any barrier; nothing but delight was hers and his, closely her arms enwrapped his body; tightly did she press her from to him in the bliss of her second surrender. She was not merely receptive now, she was eager to assist.

And her lover, overjoyed with the ardor of the young beauty desired this time to bring the passionate bliss to a still higher plane than before, gratifying his lust with the most extravagant sensations which her richly developed hips and hot temperament could be made to afford.

He advanced upon the fair girl and soon his head nestled in her cup again. He pressed his raging head upon those lips; thrills of delight again and again flowed between then, just as before, from her flushed face to the tips of her dainty feet she was happy, and in the center of all sensations, between her fine legs, seemed to rest all the blessings of paradise.

And now he told her that their passion this time must rise to greater heights than at first; and with her assistance, they would climb to the most dizzy summits of ecstasy. The young girl, already brimming with passion, listened to his words with thoughts which cannot be described. She had learned all there was to know; she did not realize that she had for her lover a man of great experience in the art of love. If there were greater delights than she had experienced the first time, she did not think she could endure them. But she determined to try and and as she found out, her powers kept her with him to the last.

He slipped his hands now under her hips, her plump. buttocks pressed heavily upon them. And now he began gently to stroke her. She put both hands around his neck. He pressed her hips tightly with his strong hands, and, at his direction, she curved her back somewhat helping to raise her hips to meet the arms. For quite a little time they did this, she thrilling with joy at every stroke. Then, as the ramming continued (it was not very happy, of course), he told how to join in it. And now, assisted by his hands, as he stroked, she lifted her hips to meet him, and soon they were rocking in blissful union. The delightful girl was quivering already with passion, but her good sense told her to be as calm as she could and enjoy it as long as nature would possibly allow. So, for many strokes, they rose and fell together, though the passion of both was steadily rising. Finally she began to cry out with the sensation; he was fearful of her passion oil flowing, and they rested.

Quiet they lay, till each was more calm when

49

he whispered to her; the observer would have seen, as Phoebus whispered, that he spread his legs somewhat, though still keeping them firmly against the chest, then he would have seen her raise her lovely legs and cross them over his, her shapely calves resting on the back of his hairy limbs, and her dainty feet together? And when he felt that sweet, smooth flesh pressing upon him a rush of passion dashed over him, and he drove his angry rod tightly into the cup of the beautiful creature; thrilled instantly by the magic pressure, she trembled in his grasp; she clung to him an instant more tightly, and then, with moans of delicious pleasure, she opened the rich fountains of her treasure house and madly poured her oil upon that straining head. Prepared for this, she did not relax so much this time as at first, but much of her strength remained. Abundantly she poured out her glorious oil, and quickly her full animation was at their mutual service.

Each knew that now the dizzy heights were to be reached.

They clung madly together at first motionless.

Well nigh crazed already by the passions each had roused in the other, they pressed their panting bodies together with immense eagerness.

More tightly, if possible, he wrapped his arms around her steaming haunches.

Nervously she slipped her arms down around the middle of his back pulling him upward upon her with all her strength.

Tighter she pressed her exquisite calves and polished legs against his straining muscles.

And when that embrace was tightest, he began to drive his rod against her cup.

It was the beginning of the mad rush to heavenly joys.

She curved her supple back, and came up with every stroke; they rocked up and down for about a score of strokes, until he knew that now IT MUST BE.

He told her what to do.

Instantly she reversed her ardent motions.

She stayed up, after she had rocked up with him, till he drew back.

Then, as he drove her, SHE CAME DOWN AGAINST HIM.

At the very first thrust, she screamed aloud.

He drew back, she moved up, his rod came within an inch of the outer gateway.

When he thrust, and she drove down to meet him, that COCK RAN NEARLY THE WHOLE

51

LENGTH OF THAT SHEATH, AND PRESSED
HER AGAINST HER SACRED LIPS.

How could any girl endure such an attack!!!

Again he drew back; again she rose, again he
came nearly to the outer lips; again he drove;
again her scream delicious agony resounded
through the room.

It was taking every conceivable effort of will-
power for him to hold off so long.

For the fourth time, he pulled back; close to
the outer opening it came; once more he rammed,
and she came to join him; once more his head
ran the torrid length of that oily sheath and
crammed hard against the cup.

She cried out harder than ever; she was sobbing, too, but with consuming passion.

Five times; back he came; forward he went;
down she came, ram it pressed heavily the tender
womb lips; her cries were maddening.

Suddenly from her crazed womb poured forth
a second spending.

But it did not weaken her.

But when he drew back the sixth time, clear
to the door, with a cry of intense agony, and
rammed it in, she did not come down to meet
him.

She was rigid with madness.

52

His head tasted her spending, and instantly sent the message to his brain, and all over his whole nervous system.

She was a beautiful demon of crazed womanhood; her whole soul was centered in her maddening sensations of passion.

Seven times he drew back; she held most, curving her back.

He rammed it the whole length of her oily cavity, with one lusty movement, and plunged its red-black head into that oil for the second time.

He understood her.

She reached down still further, she grasped his haunches; she strained her calves harder against him.

He wrapped her hips in a mighty grip, she held her lovely back in a rich curve.

She exerted every muscle of her glorious arms and legs TO PULL HIM UP HARDER AGAINST HER THIGHS.

And, in that supreme embrace, they reached the heights of paradise.

Without a preliminary throb, but with a mighty rush of scalding sperm, in the very first stroke of that maddening climax, the mighty realization of their desires was inaugurated.

With a wild cry, their very souls rushed into mutual ectasy.

They were one; they knew nothing but love, mad, mad, mad, passionate love.

Of their two bodies they were now scarcely conscious, for their whole existence centered in that sheath, where the culmination of earthly desires was being enacted.

They knew no other sensations, save those which emanated from that passion center.

He could only give short rams now, so slightly were they clasped.

But the sensations were not intermittent.

THEY WERE CONTINUOUS.

Usually, the delight in sexual union runs in waves, coincident with the thrusts of the ejaculations.

But such were their bodies, and their souls, that from the time that first immense spurt of seed was thrown upon that already exquisitely tortured cup, the sensation of curstrial joy, supreme pleasure, superb intensity of passion, exalted delight of possession, mad delight of realization, the crazed delirium of the union of two such ardent souls, NEVER CEASED, TILL LONG AFTER THE MIGHTY RUSH OF PASSION FROM THE LUSTY LOINS OF PHOEBUS INTO THE GLO-

54

RIOUS BODY OF ESMERALDA HAD ENDED
ITS MAGNIFICENT FLOW! ! ! ! ! !

And now we must leave the lovely Esmeralda
and the handsome Phoebus to pass the remainder
of the night. We have not time to relate, how,
after this supreme encounter of passion, they lay
long in each other's arms, enjoying innocent conversation. Both were wearied by that mighty
convulsion of their mutual passion, and Phoebus
knew, too, that the way to win a repetition of
favors is not to urge them too frequently. But
before they finally disposed themselves to sleep,
their desires reasserted themselves and they again
went to heaven together. Then the now tired,
but not satiated, girl fell asleep, and he soon
joined her.

But when the next morning's sun aroused them
both at once, each looked with delight upon the
nudity of the other, and it was not long till interest turned to desire. Her eyes sparkled as she
saw his tool raise its head proudly, as he gazed
upon her naked charms, and, after taking a good
look at her vanquisher by daylight, she was nothing loathe to be gathered in her lover's arms,
and have that ugly monster concealed from the
light within the eagerly encircling sheath of her
fair form.

When that charming act was accomplished,
they arose and began to pick up their scattered
garments which the haste of the night before
had left where they might fall. And it took so
long to find everything and playfully to begin to
dress that his tool became erect again. And she
in her chemisette and one flimsy skirt, murmured
not when he playfully therw her back on the bed,
just as she was, opened the chemise and let her
glorious bubbies out, to press his still naked bosom, threw her thin skirt up to her waist, and
buried his amorous rod once more in her delighted
cavity; and there, in that unconventional manner,
they clung together, until nature had had her
own sweet way again, with loving Phoebus and
lovely Esmeralda.

And how many times this blissful tale was repeated, during the long friendship of those two,
I must leave you to guess.

Memories

Y CHILDHOOD was a very dull one. I am hardly certain whether I remember my mother or not.

Till about ten years of age my life was passed in almost claustial loneliness. I lived in a large rambling two storied house with my father and his aunt. My father however was almost always absent and besides he took very little notice of us when he was at home. My aunt got up very late and I hardly ever saw her before dinner time at half past one. I had some toys but no playmate. I was so pampered with dainties, surfeited with sweet meats but as I took no exercise I had no appetite especially for wholesome food, would have.

My days, withal flowed on monotonously had it not been for an informity of mine, which really tortured my life. I was terribly frightened of poodles. I did not care much for any dogs in general, but at the sight of a poodle, I grew deathly pale, I trembled from head to foot, and almost fainted from fear. Still I could hardly call it fear, it was more a kind of loathsomeness, that made me thoroughly sick.

I have been told that my mother, during her pregnancy, had been frightened by a poodle that my aunt had at the time and that died shortly afterwards, still can such a circumstance produce so great an impression on the foetus in the earlier stages of gestation? And yet I cannot explain this infirmity otherwise.

As I grew older I tried to reason myself out of this dislike and I have almost succeeded in overcoming it; now I can even bear the sight of one of these canine clowns.

I have very few recollections of those early years, and those I have are hardly worth recording. Still it is astounding how some triling facts sink deeply into a child's mind and are never forgotten, whilst many important events pass entirely into oblivion.

When I was about four or five years of age, I was, as usual, playing alone with some blocks of wood. In the same room there was a young dressmaker, busy at one of my aunt's gowns. This girl, who must have been rather pretty—was about 18 or 19, for she was engaged at the time and married shortly afterwards.

As I was playing the dressmaker stopped in her work and looked at me. She was flushed, her eyes were sparkling and her lips were very red.

Come here, said she, you are a good boy, are you not?

Yes, I replied indifferently.

Come then and give me a kiss; I am very fond of good boys.

I looked at her astonished.

Come on, repeated she, with a husky voice. I at last went up to her. She caught my face between both her hands and kissed me repeatedly and lingeringly on my mouth with eagerness.

As you are a very good boy, tomorrow I'll bring you some bonbons, she said. Do you know where I keep my sweeties?

No, I replied.

Well, come nearer, my pet, and I'll show you,— her voice was trembling.

I shuffled up to her. She took hold of my hand and held it tightly by the wrist, then opening her legs wide apart and uplifting her skirts, she thrust my little fist between her thighs and pressed it deep between her soft warm flesh.

I don't think there are many comfits there to-day but look well, perhaps you might find one or two, and you are such a clever little boy.

I was both astonished and shy; although I could not have given any reason for it, still I instinctively felt that it was a naughty thing to do. I was therefore going to draw my hand away, but curiosity retained me.

What I touched was at the same time warm, pulpy and moist, nay the further my hand was plunged in, the more intense the heat grew.

Moreover to my utter surprise there was a lot of hair growing over her stomach and all around that sticky flesh.

My bewilderment increased when after a greater exploration I found that she had no birdie, or a little bag with balls but that she had a beard instead.

In the meanwhile, always holding me by my arm, she rubbed my little fist in the hot place— always telling me in a husky panting voice to look for sweeties, till I felt it get quite wet.

I asked her what she was doing, if she was piddling on my hand, but she began to pant and to squeeze my arm tightly. Ah! she said, with a sigh of satisfaction, I've done it, it was very nice, wasn't it?

Do you like the smell? she said, putting my hand under my nose.

I do not know what I answered but I remember

it smelt fishy and I smelt it over and over all that day. I never forgot it, and now whenever that smell of a woman's coynte mounts to my nostrils, I always remember the girl I masturbated.

Haven't I a funny pussy, said she, should you like to see it, my dear?

I don't thing I answered her anything but I certainly started with very round eyes.

At that moment there was a sound of footsteps, for she said to me:

If you are a very bood boy, I'll show you my pussy another time. Only mind it's a secret and as you are a little man, you must never tell secrets. Tomorrow I'll bring you some bon bons. Now go and play. Saying this she pushed me away and resumed her sewing.

I went back to my toys; I smelt my hand and played.

For a long time I wondered whether women really had a real pussy between their legs; being fond of cats, I would like to see it.

Shortly after this event there happened another one, which—although I have not exactly cherished it—I could never forget for erotic words and subjects seem to cling with a particular tenacity to a child's mind.

It was a hot summer day and I was lounging listlessly in the hall downstairs, the door of which —opening on the street, was ajar. My aunt had gone to vespers.

In the hall, over the door opposite the entrance was a huge stuffed vulture perched with outstretched wings on a stand.

All at once as I was playing I turned and saw two boys standing at the door, looking at the bird and making as I thought all kinds of irrelevant remarks about it and laughing.

I advanced and ordered the two vagrants out of the house.

Is it your house? said the elder mockingly.

Of course I said sternly.

A marmot who has a house of his own, said the younger.

Out from here, said I.

Your house? continued the big boy cynically, then taking his pizzle out of his ragged breeches and shaking it, this is yours, baby, and you can come and suck it if you like.

You have bought the house with this, said the other boy imitating the example of his friend and splitting with laughter, haven't you, baby?

I rushed at them in a mad rage and they fled before my fury.

I felt myself humiliated and burst into a fit of hysteric sobs. And even when my aunt brought me new boots, I did not want to keep them on.

After a few days I managed to get over the loathsomeness of the affair.

Another fact that also impressed me at the time was the peculiar copulation of a dog and a bitch. I happened to be at the dining room window when I witnessed the astounding sight.

Our house—as you know—overlooked a kind of yard and as its inmates always afforded me great interest, I passed many hours of the day watching them.

It therefore happened, at the time I speak of that the owner of one of the booths possessed a dog, a peculiar animal with many long pointed breasts—which I could not help noticing, as it was ever pestered by all the curs of the neighborhood. One day as I went to the window I saw that and another dog, tied together—as I imagined—by their tails and they could not get free from one another.

The two pitiable animals were howling for the children were throwing stones at them.

It was a rare sight so I called everybody to hasten and enjoy it. As soon as my nurse perceived the two dogs, she snatched me up, cuffed

me soundly, sent me off from the window, and told
me if I ever looked upon such things again, my
eyes would drop out of my head.

I therefore began pondering. Why was I a
naughty boy? Perhaps the dogs had not been
tied, perhaps I ruminated they had stuck their
tails into each other's bottoms, just for fun; that
of course would not have been a thing to be looked
at. It was a riddle which I only solved many
years afterwards.

At about ten my father sent me to school. Never having had any playmates of my own age, I
was shy as a girl and on that account mercilessly
plagued and made fun of. The little boys called
me Madamoiselle and the big ones tormented me.
They used to clasp me from behind and clasping
me, they began bumping the middle part against
my bum, asking me how I liked it. I did not of
course understand what they were hinting at.

After some time I got to be great friends with
one of my schoolfellows and he then explained
to me what those horrible boys wanted to do. It
was he who informed me one day, as a great secret, that girls had no birdie as we had.

No, of course they haven't, quoth I, proud to
show my knowledge, they have a pussy instead.

He burst into laughter.

64

Shortly after this confab, we happened to be in his garden behind a hedge of bushes, discussing erotic subjects.

Hearing his younger sister's voice, he called her to him, then catching hold of her, he threw her on the grass, lifted up her skirts, opened her drawers, showed me the rosy flesh between her thighs that tiny cleft bordered by two pale lips like a long mouth, which contorted into grimaces as she tried to free herself from his clutches.

He however sat astraddle on her stomach and with the tips of his fingers opened the lips. I sank down on my knees and looked within, astonished to see the numerous folds of living flesh.

Put your finger in and see how moist it feels, said he.

I should, in fact, have liked to continue my explorations but the girl began to screech so loud that we had to let her go.

From that day, with other girls and boys of our own age, we often compared notes, we measured whose pizzle was the thickest and the longest, whose unhooded most and above all who could piss the farthest and the highest.

Another delightful thing was to get some girl to lie across our knees, to open her pants and slap her buttocks till it made our hands as well as those quiescent globes red as poppies, hot as ovens and tingle with pain; still we found an inexplainable pleasure in the sound cuffs we gave, for it almost made our tiny prickles stand on an end. This amusement however was the beginning and the cause of all my troubles in after-life.

One day we were interrupted in the very midst of our sport. I remember all the details of the scene. It was a warm spring day; we were in our favorite secluded nook.

My schoolmate was squatted on the sod, having his sister's friend across his knees. He had lifted up her white petticoats, pulled open her cambric pants and exhibited two rounded lobes of flesh, like a large melon cut in two, only that the color was a faint pinkish tint.

To our delight he opened the two lobes widely apart and thus discovered the little brownish dot of her tiny hole and forthwith tried to force his finger into it. The aperture was however too small, and as he thrust his index brutally within it, the poor child screamed with pain.

Sotte, said he, and pulling out his finger, he gave her such a smacking slap that the white flesh was at once flushed, leaving the incarnadine sign of his five fingers. The first blow had been too strong and unexpected; the girl uttered a faint cry at which we all clapped our hands in high glee.

Ah! you are mewing, are you, said the boy excited, and he immediately gave her another and much stronger slap. The girl uttered a shriller cry, at which we all capered for joy, in a kind of wild dance.

All at once my friend's eldest sister, a girl of 18, appeared arm in arm with the young man to whom she was engaged at one end of the flowery path. On the other outlet we saw an old aunt —a prim weazened spinster—who always looked upon us as a hellish brood.

Fancy how sheepish and crestfallen we looked as we held our little pizzles in our hand and pissed as high as we possibly could.

My friend was whipped before us—we his friends were sent home in disgrace.

I was soundly thrashed by my father, lectured by my aunt and scolded by my nurse.

After a few days at home, my aunt persuaded my father to send me as a boarder in some school.

I had hitherto dabbled in early vice thoughtlessly and without malice. In that hotbed of rottenness—a French boarding school—I soon learnt all the secrets of life and still, strange to say, it was not by my schoolfellows.

For several reasons I was not placed in the dormitory with the other boys. First I was very young and second my story having been related to the head master, he had been requested to keep sharp lookout on my morals; for I was described as a black sheep with the very worst propensities.

I was therefore put to sleep with one of the nurses, a stout masculine looking woman, past the canonocal age. A screen however divided the room into two compartments.

One sultry summer night I awoke feeling very hot and feverish parched with thirst, I got up to see if I could find a glass of water. There was no water on my night table and I crossed over to her side to see if I could find any there. The nurse was lying on her back, her legs almost apart, her thighs opened, her slit uplifted.

All her middle parts were entirely bare. In that pale amber light her skin loooked as white and smooth as ivory. I should almost have felt inclined to pass my hand over it had not my eyes fallen at once, on the dark fleece, which covered half of her thighs and almost reached up to her navel.

I stared at her with wide opened eyes. This woman possessed a pussy and no mistake about it.

As the nurse was sound asleep and snoring loudly, I passed my hand lightly, tremblingly over the long hair. It seemed to grow there. All at once the nurse gave a kind of snort, moved and her hand came down on mine. I slipped away my hand, popped down quickly and crawled noiselessly under the bed.

Guillaume, said she, stretching out, I believe, her arms in her sleep, where are you?

Of course I gave no answer. By tne noise the bed made, I knew she had turned on the other side.

I was about to leave my hiding place, when I heard a slight noise; some one was actually turning the handle of the door. It opened without creaking.

Lying flat on my stomach, I could see the legs of a barefooted man, standing on the threshold.

At first I thought it was a burglar. The man came close to the side of the bed and stopped for a minute.

What was he doing? My heart was giving some mighty thumps. Perhaps he was smothering the nurse with her own bolster. Presently I heart a sound but it was very much like a kiss then another, and still another.

No, I could not be mistaken.

Oh! Guillaume, is it you, so you're come. Thereupon she moved on one side, as if she was making
place for him.

I thought, she has been expecting him. Who
could he be?

In the whole house there were several Guillaumes, one of the older boys, one of the junior
boys, one of the junior masters, and a sturdy Auvergnat of a servant man were all Williams, which
of them was the conqueror? Moreover was he so
very fond of this old virago that he stealthily
crept into her room like a thief only to kiss her?

Whilst I was lost in these surmises, I saw his
bare legs and feet disappear and by the noise of
the mattress—evidently crushed down, I guessed
that Guillaume had got into the matron's bed.

A moment's silence followed; a more expert ear
might have detected the straining of muscles, the
clasping of naked flesh; mine did not. Then succeeded a suppressed smacking of kisses, together
with an interrupted conversation in hushed and
husky tones.

What could they be talking about? I strained
my ears but could not catch the slightest syllable.

Soon the mattresses were set in motion, to
which a slight and almost musical creaking of the
bedstead kept time. It was now a regular cadence

70

of bumping and plunging, something like a continuous kneading of dough, marked at intervals by a sound like that of a horse's hood drawn out of the mire.

My wildest conjectures were too vague to allow me to form any plausible supposition as to what they were about.

Little by little the bucking and pounding as well as the creaking increased both in time as well as in strength. I was dreadfully frightened lest the whôle bedstead would come down upon me and crush me. I therefore crept to the farthermost end of the bed and kept ready to slip out if the slightest accident happened.

When there, I heard the nurse whisper to Guillaume to take care lest he might wake the marmot—that was me—with the noise he was making.

The devil take the brat, muttered the conqueror, it was time he was got out of your room.

Thereupon the bumps and thuds increased, then a puffing and panting, intermingled with grunts of satisfaction and wriggles which seemed more of pleasure than of pain, together with an indescribable gurgling.

Then in a suppressed sotto voce: There I'm doing it, ah! louder, shudderingly—I'm doing it,

ah! and after a slight pause, he added in a more
tremulous and louder voice—ah! I've done it.
Then some panting, a few seconds of silence during which I asked myself what Guillaume had
done—and he added with ineffable satisfaction:

Ah! futtering is after all the only thing worth
living for in this world.

How those words impressed me. I repeated
them over and over to myself.

I had found out what Guillaume and the nurse
were doing. They were futtering. Yes, but what
was futtering?

I had hitherto believed that futter meant to
thrash a person, but evidently it was not that.

After a lengthy pause the man added: But did
you not enjoy it?

Now that Guillaume spoke in his natural voice,
I was all but certain that it was the junior master.

The matron said: No, since that sacred brat
had been put in my room, I never feel at ease,
and all my fun is spoiled.

Oh, he always sleeps like a top.

I'm not quite so sure of that, he's such a little
sneak. Just before you came in, I was sure I felt
a hand on my coynte.

How I pricked my ears up at the word. That
was a coynte then and not a pussy.

Nothing; only I thought it was you.

Oh, you must have been dreaming.

Yes, I suppose so.

After that they kissed, then the bed creaked again and she added:

You had better go away at once, it is late.

Some more kissing took place, then he jumped down, and said:

Ta ta—on Wednesday next, said he and then crept away on tiptoe.

I waited just a little and heard the nurse snore and then crept on all fours to my bed.

It was late when I woke, nay the nurse was tugging at me to rouse me from my overpowering drowsiness.

I stared at her and she seemed for a moment quite abashed.

Why are you looking at me so surprised, she asked.

Oh, I think I must have been dreaming.

About what? my pretty pet!

I . . . I don't think I remember.

Come, you are a darling of a child, do try and think what it was.

I paused for a moment and then encouraged by her loving words, and prompted by the curiosity that I felt:

Mrs. Lachand, said I, with a fluttering heart and a trembling voice.

Well, and then, asked Guillaume.

Well, my love.

Please, will you tell me what futtering is?

I shall never forget the transformation that woman's face underwent. From sweet benevolent cozening look, it changed into the ugliest of grim scowls.

She lifted up her hand and gave me a smacking slap, then in a hissing undertone said:

You dirty sneaking wretch, ah! you want to know what futtering is, well, I'll show you.

Thereupon she turned me on my back and pulling up my night gown she began to thrash me mercilessly, nay the more she struck the greater pleasure she felt, and the smarter were the blows she gave.

Now I hope you've been futtered to your heart's content, and it'll be a long while before you ask me such a question again; next time I won't thrash you, I'll simply take you by your ear and drag you to the head master. We all know what a filthy imp you were when you came to us, so he'll expell you from school at once.

Of course I was sobbing piteously, so she took

me several times to make me stop, then she began scolding again.

Her scolding and my whimpering were both suddenly stopped by the sound of the drum. It was the second signal so I ought to have already been combed, washed and ready to join my school fellows.

The nurse soused my head in a basin of water, anxiously bidding me at the same time to forget the terrible word I uttered and that for this time she would not speak to the masters, then she helped me put on my dirty uniform.

The day dragged on wearily and I was listless and muddled and utterly depressed.

In my despondency, I was glad when night came on, my bed was a real haven of rest. Although I intended to remain awake, just to see if anything would happen, still, no sooner was my head on the pillow, then I went off to sleep.

I only slumbered lightly for I woke when the matron came in and again I woke when she wallowed in her bed. As in a dream I heard the clock strike one, then I was conscious of a slight noise, the door of the room was opened and some one came in.

In spite of all my curiosity I durst not turn

around, nor move; I felt sure the matron would be listening to hear if I was awake.

In fact she soon uttered a low hissing sound and she jumped out of her bed.

She stopped the man and then went over to my bed. I was lying flat on my stomach, my face turned to the wall, as quiet as a mouse. I knew she had come to make sure that I was asleep and she patted me lightly and asked me if I wanted to do pi-pi but seeing that I did not budge but breathed softly and slowly, she thought I was asleep and went back to Guillaume.

As soon as they were together, they began to whisper in the same low husky somewhat nasal tones. By degrees they got more excited and their tones grew louder and as I listened it seemed to me that the man's voice was that of another Guillaume, a senior scholar, a young Marseillais of about 17, the sturdiest fellow of the whole school.

They seemed to be enjoying their little game. I turned my head as much as I could and strained my eyes to their corners.

They were now standing close together, kissing. She was holding his pizzle and—I think—rubbing it. He had uplifted her shift and his hand was between her legs.

76

After they had been amusing themselves in this way for a while, they both disappeared behind the screen, and it was evident they had gone to bed together.

They first proceeded quietly like a steam engine, just started, but after a few strokes, the speed of the piston rod increased rapidly.

It was the same thumping and bumping, the same inarticulate sounds of puffing, of breathing painfully and panting pleasurably even the same hoarse gurglings, to which the thuds on the mattress the creaking of the hinges the straining of the wooden bed kept time.

Evidently they were having their fill of pleasure —for surely they would not take so much trouble for nothing—and I therefore concluded they were doing the thing worth living for.

My curiosity had risen to such a pitch of excitement that I could hardly keep still any longer, my craving to see them futtering was irresistible.

My first plan was to slip on the floor quetly and go and peep round the screen, but on second thought I concluded it would be better to stand on the bed and look over that partition of paper.

I therefore got up quietly, holding myself as well as I could to the wall and making as little

noise as possible, as I was very light, the bed did
not make the slightest sound.

For a little while I could not understand much
of what I saw but by degrees I perceived that the
matron was lying on her back and Guillaume was
on top of her. They were both moving up and
down.

Straining my eyes, holding my breath, I advanced cautiously towards the edge of the bed.
I now saw that she had her fat legs entwined in
his, whilst both were clasped in each other's arms.

There, there, said she, move a little, but don't
pull yourself up, there, like that, push it in as
far as you can, ah!

In my eagerness to see, I bent just a little forwards when—all at once—the mattress gave way
under my feet and lo! I slipped and fell with a
tremendous thud on the floor.

Although I hurt my head and bruised my back,
I durst not utter a moan, still I could not help
whimpering a little as I tried to extricate myself
from the sheet, but before I could get up the matron was by my side, clapping her hand on my
mouth and almost smothering me, for fear I might
scream.

What's the matter with you, you little monster?
she hissed in my ear.

78

I . . . I fell out of my bed.

Oh, you fell, you toad, and catching hold of my hair she shook me violently—and how did you manage to do that, pray?

I think I slipped, I answered gasping.

In your sleep? said she relenting.

Yes, I think I was dreaming.

Oh, you were dreaming, poor dear, were you? added she in a soothing voice, kissing me.

Thereupon she helped me to get back into bed, she tucked me and then bade me go off to sleep.

I had seen what I wanted, though not perhaps not quite as much as I should have liked; of course I could not go off to sleep after that.

For a while they kept very silent then—after some time—I heard the matron come up to my bed. I did exactly what I had done before. She called me by name. I did not vouchsafe any answer. She then went back to her bed.

Now you had better go, said she gruffly.

Oh, let me slip it in once more, rejoined he coaxingly.

No, no, not tonight.

Oh, but that cursed toad spoiled everything just as I was going to shoot.

I asked myself what he was going to shoot?

No, said the matron, it's useless, but I'll tell

you what if you like, you can faire minette to me, that can be done noiselessly.

This was a new wonder to me. What were they going to do? I did wish they would let me join in their little game. I durst not move any more for I felt sure their rage would be ungovernable if I spoilt their fun a second time.

What ever their game they kept it quiet for some time, then there was some wriggling and wallowing, a great deal of strong breathing, the nurse seemed to be having stomach ache, then a subdued sighing as if the pain was over and all was silent for a few minutes.

Thereupon I think they rose.

Did you enjoy it? quote he.

Fichtre! in a decided tone.

I did it nicely, didn't I?

Very.

Then—some low words in a longing tone which I could not understand.

Go away you pig, answered she.

Then on Friday?

Yes.

He thereupon went to her basin and seemed to be rinsing his mouth.

For some evenings I slept soundly. I never heard anything, never woke at all. I had, I think caught cold, a very slight cold indeed, for I did not perceive it, but the matron who had grown exceedingly fond of me, said that I coughed in the night and that I breathed with a wheezing sound so she made me take a cup of tea before going to bed.

It was very good and sweet, she said, but I was not to mention it to the other boys for they would be jealous. I kept taking it for several nights, but whether it was my cold or the sultry hot days, the more I slept the more drowsy I grew.

At last, about a fortnight later—having gotten sick of my tisane and being sure that I had neither a cold nor a cough any more, I—the matron not mounting guard—instead of drinking it and having it pass through my body into the vessel into which it was destined to go, I deftly poured it into the night vase at once.

I went off to sleep, but I did not fall into that lethargy of the evening before.

In the middle of the night I had a peculiar dream. I was on board of a ship and the matron was with me, but I do not exactly know whether we were in bed or not.

All at once the waves began to roll high and dash against the bow of the ship that laboring to make headway through the trough of the waters.

She was straining her bulwarks and the engine was puffing madly and the piston rod going in and out of the cylinder. All at once the ship was attacked by pirates—just like in the story I had been reading that very evening—only one of them had got over the matron, as Guillaume Chretien had done a fortnight ago, and she, poor thing was sobbing and calling for help. Yes, I could hear her plainly, she was panting, wallowing, almost screeching.

I thereupon seized a crowbar and ran to her help. Some one had rung the bell, the ship was afire, I shrieked for help, I yelled.

There was a scuffle. The nurse was by my side, almost throttling me, her eyes were out of her head, her hair all disheveled, she was looking like a devil. A man appeared likewise by my bed.

If you scream, you dirty blackguard, I'll just murder you.

The nurse gagged me. I now recognized the man that had thus threatened me. It was Guillaume, the broad shouldered Auvergnat servant man. Another second and he vanished behind the screen.

A few moments afterwards there were lights and footsteps in the passage but the door being locked no one could come in. The nurse told them however that there was nothing the matter with me, I had been dreaming and pulled the bell rope in my sleep; so they all went off grumbling and evidently cursing me as giving more trouble than the whole school together.

I was shaken and thumped and ordered to go to sleep at once which I tried to do as quickly as possible.

My stay in that boarding school was however to be of slight duration.

Not long after the incident of that night, Mr. Durieux, one of the Guillaumes who had slept and enjoyed my matron so much one evening that I remembered, was explaining to us something about the Persian wars.

The subject was an interesting one and I remember him saying that lads of 15 and 16 fought like heroes.

All at once the boy next to me whispered in my ear:

Just ask him at what age can one fire off a shot!

Why, rejoined I innocently.

Just for the fun of the thing, ask him, unless you are frightened.

I protested that I was not and I did as I was bid, simply straightforwardly.

I saw Mr. Durieux blush scarlet and bounce off his chair as if he had been jerked out of it. The whole class burst into a loud fit of laughter.

M. Durieux glared at me, and ordered silence. Leave the class, he then said to me.

But why? said I trembling.

Will you go at once, you scoundrel, or I'll call Guillaume.

I knew that Guillaume, in fact all three Guillaumes bore me a grudge. Had I not interrupted them all when they were futtering the matron and at a time when they were at the height of emotion. I rose at once, therefore, hoping that he

But as I never saw any of the boys and was expelled from school, it was not until I was grown up that I finally knew that the biggest thing in life was fucking. As I grew older I realized that fucking is life itself; so applying my mind to writing that you may benefit, I now endeavor to write the following short stories.

FLORENCE

INETEEN, dainty, but not slender, with rosy cheeks, and brightest shining eyes, vivacious, jolly; she was, in short, wholly attractive; a girl whom the best of men might love, and, on the other hand, one whose round form less than a saint might long to fondle. For two years she had been employed in the office of M——& C, away down town in New York City; and for a long time had the junior partner, Mr. Thompson, admired her beauty and grace, not to say, in Summer, the exquisite, white roundness of her pretty arms and that glimpse of her charming neck. But he was sensible, and simply admired her, took pains to conceal it; and so time passed.

But in September, 1919, a new office boy came to the firm. He was a bright young fellow, a well-knit boy, good looking and brim full of health. His youthful vigor seemed to cast a glow over the entire office, which, of course, Miss Florence noted as did all the rest. But none but she felt it as deeply. There was something about the boy that made her thrill gently whenever he was near her, and when his hand touched hers, accidentally or otherwise, she seemed to feel a distinct electric shock. Horace did not attempt to conceal his liking for her, though to what extent he hoped to advance in her favors only he could have told. A month passed; they seemed to be more attracted to each other daily. And by the first of December, the girl used to find some excuse to be the last one in the office (the rest left about half past four), and she and Horace used to visit with much pleasure. Their attraction for each other could not be stationary, of course, and ere long she used to let the sturdy youth take her in his arms and hug her closely, and then to kiss her repeatedly, which gave her more pleasure than she would have admitted. Perhaps she thought he was only a child, but in this she was much mistaken.

Now she became bolder, so that there was no mistaking his desires, and she would often make up her mind to break off with him altogether, and then when night came, she would find herself in his embraces once more, saying to herself, after that pleasure, that tomorrow would be different. And so one day came, when, after they were left alone, he coaxed her to go to another room with him, where he said he had a bottle of cider. She thought of nothing wrong and went with him, and found herself in the place she had never been before, a bedroom used by the night floorwalker, after his duties at midnight were over. She was a little frightened at first, but the young man really did have a bottle of cider, and they drank some. Of course there was nothing wrong about this fact, but there must have been a little of something else in it. At any rate it made her head a little giddy, and still thinking nothing improper, she lay down upon the floor walker's bed.

Now, whether the boy had had this in mind, or simply that the sight of the lovely girl lying there stimulated his desires, I do not now. I know, however, that he quickly came to the bedside, and, while she seemed not to be aware of what was taking place, he gently raised her skirts, until her round, plump calves, with their soft black stockings, were exposed; and after an instance of excited admiration he quickly got on the bed, and ran his hand up under her clothes. Before she could prevent he pressed and tickled her between her thighs in a way that made her cry out with excitement. Try as she would then,

she could not get his hand away, for as soon as
her strength would be roused to repulse him, he
would again tickle and press her, and all her power would be lost through that delightful sensation on that unaccustomed spot. And with each
attack her powers of resistance grew less, till finally within five minutes after she had fallen upon
the bed, she lay there with his hand still under
her clothing, absolutely helpless, trembling all
over with nervous excitement, and between her
legs an indescribable sensation, which she had
never felt before.

And now, when she fell back helpless, and lay
still, he knew that she was his. She did not
even turn her head when he leaped off the bed
and tore off his pants, exposing his lusty rod,
stiff as a red hot poker. She hardly moved a
hand when he boldly climbed on the bed again,
raised both her skirts to her waist, and in feverish haste unfastened her drawers. She only cried
out, but did not stir when he pulled those drawers
down and off, exposing the matchless whiteness
of her polished legs, so round and charming, and
between them that dainty dove's nest. The sight
of her virgin whiteness inspired the boy to no
pity; he quickly planted himself between those
ivory columns, he bunted his head against her

sanctuary for a few times, then, seizing it with his eager hand, he found the spot, inserted its end into the sheath, and there, before she was hardly conscious of his crime, she found herself impaled upon the tool of that devilish ruffian, she would have been a prize of the gods themselves.

Her maidenhood gone, she offered not the slightest resistance to his onslaught, and scarcely had he penetrated to the citadel of love when she spent all over him, in the exuberance of her nature. He felt it, and gloating over his prize, prepared to do the act quickly. Even yet some one might have saved her from this shame, but, alas, succor came too late. For it was not until he had given her several rams of his lusty tool, that there was sound of a key being put in the lock of the outer door; he heard, but nothing would stop him; stiffly he stroked her; now his rod tightened; there was a great throb of the lecherous muscle. Then the door opened, a man rushed into the room, took in the situation at a glance, ran to the bed, grabbed the vile youth by the hips, and pulled him away.

But the poor girl's ruin was accomplished, for while Mr. Thompson was hurrying across the long room, the youth had squirted a charge of seed upon her pure lips, and now, as the angry employer jerked him away, his sperm still spurted in jets from his stiff rod. But quickly with blows and curses, did the infuriated Thompson throw the fellow out of the room, with warning never to let him see his face again.

And now the poor ruined girl was left alone with the man who had admired her so long, and whom she, too, had secretly admired. Instinctively she had lowered her skirts, but she was too much excited to attempt to flee; she remained motionless. Mr. Thompson then came to the bedside, sat down by her, and tried to calm her by not appearing to think of what had happened. But, honorable though her friend was, the vision of those exquisite legs and the deep flush of excitement still covered her pretty cheeks, troubling him greatly. Let us tell the whole truth and say that, try as he would, the recollection of that sight forced itself so often upon his mind that soon he had an erection as great as Horace's, who had actually reached that haven of desire, though only for an instant.

He stretched himself on the bed; he had locked and bolted the door, before he came back; he lay at a distance from her; she did not object to his lying there; in fact, it seemed to him that her moist eyes were becoming alluring. Nature had, in truth, been roused in her. And finally he could no longer keep down his rising feelings, and began to talk of what he had seen. And at last, to be certain that anything had come from that scoundrel's rod to pollute the lovely girl, he openly asked her that question. She read his thoughts, and blushed still deeper when she replied, "Yes, Mr. Thompson, only one stroke; but that was enough; I felt it, and I am not a virgin any longer."

In a flash he clasped her close in his strong arms.

"Oh dearest Florence, you know I would never have done this act to you; your purity would have always been safe with me. But now, if it is gone, and you surely know if his seed did touch you, if it has, then come and lie in my arms, and we will love to the very heights of heaven."

And what could the delighted girl say, but to murmur "Yes," blushing ever deeper.

With a cry of pleasure, he sprang off the bed, he kissed her pretty eyes shut, warning her not to open then until he should tell her she might. Then he quickly tore off his every garment, and his fine, white body, and muscular back, arms and legs were a glorious sight. She was blissful as

she heard the rustling of his clothing; she knew
real happiness was rapidly approaching.

Then he came to the bed, tool lustily standing;
she kept her eyes closed as he wished. "Don't
be frightened, sweetheart," he said and gently
began to remove her shoes; quickly they were
off, and her stockings soon followed. Then he
gently raised her up; she understood and herself
unfastened her collar; then her waist was an easy
matter. Now he raised her to her feet; taking
care that her hands should not feel his naked
flesh; her two skirts came down easily around
her shapely form; then her girdle; and then her
rather long chemise. The beauty's eyes were still
closed; she felt no fear though she knew she was
nearly naked.

He could not refrain from a cry of delight, as
he paused a moment and gazed at her beautifully
turned legs, her supple, not to say voluptuous
hips, where lay heaven itself. Then, with trembling hands, he raised her flimsy shift; he uncov-
ered her snow white belly with its deep navel,
then he came to the luscious barrier of her
breasts, where he had to make a considerable effort to raise the garment over them without
pressing his hands against her glorious hillocks,
with their already erect nipples.

92

"Now raise your arms, darling," says he.

She does so, up he slips the garment over their beautiful white roundness, and the wonderful girl is naked.

He takes her by the hand, and tells her to lie down on the bed, whispering to her to lie back a little way upon it, which she quickly does. The room seems to be aglow with passionate desire.

He stands for an instant more and gazes at the exquisite, bare, white form lying there, already so delighted, and soon to be fairly crazed with delirious passion.

Then he bids her open her eyes; she does so.

She sees for the first time his well-knit, white form, with gloriously stiff standing yard; she almost faints for an instant, with the rush of many thoughts, then passion overcomes all else, she stretches both lovely arms toward him; he instantly climbs upon the bed; she half rises to meet his embrace, they wrap their arms about each other passionately and sink down together. moaning out their delight as they press their glowing forms tightly against each other, while those luscious hillocks, which never before felt man's touch, thrill with the sensation.

No mortal can describe such sensations. So all we can say is that they lay there a long time, simply drinking in the sweet delight of each other's flesh. Locked in that embrace they mutually sighed and moaned out their extremes of pleasure.

And so gradually, but steadily, did their longing increase for further joys, and so mutually did they act, that they hardly noticed the degrees by which they slowly turned, till he was stretched upon the exquisite form of the happy creature as she lay flat on her back. His body matched hers perfectly. Cheek pressed against cheek, shoulders matched shoulders, breasts pressed breasts, and true it was, though strange, that the fully erect nipples on her luscious hillocks kissed exactly the little nipples on his bosom, and seemed to create, by that very contact, a gentle current of pleasure through each other. Belly matched belly as they lay; his legs extended exactly on top of her lovely round columns, until his firm built feet gently clasped her dainty, white ones between them. And, best of all, his rod stood gloriously stiff, straight upward between their bellies, and his big balls hung just below the beginning of that hairy nest in which was her already burning lips, showing just how they would lie when the lovers were united in true love.

For a long, delightful time they lay in that

position, neither speaking. The divine kiss of her perfumed flesh was for some time satisfaction.

But after a time, that very divinity of sex inspired him to the consummation of the matchless act; his passion, like hers, was now imporiously demanding full satisfaction of every sense, which the coupling of their matchless bodies together should soon produce in both.

So, at length, he gently pressed his feet between those dainty ones of hers; her round, white calves bade each other good bye; her knees gave each other their last token; and, finally, her round, full thighs kissed each the other's velvet fulness and separated; those lovely charms were' not to be united again till the very heights of heaven had been attained by their lovely mistress, in the mossy nest which their parting now left exposed to the welcome thrust of that throbbing rod, which had so long knocked for admission to its sacred portals.

Still neither spoke, when the outpost of the citadel was now unprotected. Both sighed in mutual delight; once more cheek pressed cheek, shoulder pressed shoulder, breasts kissed breasts; she was now, oh, so eager to give. Then his careful hand sought, found, guided. This was of course, not new to her, but, oh, how much sweeter at even this first approach. And as his rod surely, but slowly and carefully, entered her moist sheath, it seemed to her as if magnetism thrilled from it already. Gradually he advanced until he nestled its head against her womb.

Instantly a current of electricity was established; the delighted girl felt it, and quivered in pleasure; he felt it too, and was as joyed as she. Entirely still then they lay, drinking in, without motion, each other's internal delights, as previously they had feasted on the pleasures of flesh alone.

And soon the alternating stream of magnetism, so much desired and so seldom felt, now began to flow between them. Suddenly he felt of warmth flowing into his cock; it filled it, and then he clearly felt it run in his spine to his brain. There for a brief period it burned and fire flashed before his eyes; he could see nothing else. Then swiftly down it went again to his tool, and he distinctly felt it running into her womb. Then she, in turn, thrilled as she felt her whole womb quiver with that current of delight, up then it rushed to her brain; her brain reeled with the shock and she was in lurid delight while it lasted. Then, finally, down it hurried again, and crowded into his horn.

Thus this continued again and each time it

seemed more entrancing. In absolute stillness they lay, while this steadily increasing current of magnetism flowed back and forth.

Four delicious times it passed from her to him; four times, each intensified it ran from the point of his rod, clasped by her inner lips into her womb.

Now she felt this was the last she could possibly endure, as for the fifth time she poured its magnetic strength into his cock. And he felt it that fifth time, while it rushed as before to his head it left in his balls a stinging sensation that almost overcame him at once. Vivid lights flashed before his eyes, his brain seemed on fire, intoxicating perfume rose from her body now profusely sweating with passion.

Now a final rush of that flame down his spine; his horn seemed fairly to shoot out a flame as the fiery glow poured into her womb, she felt it coming, and thought she would surely faint, but, oh, a thousand joys, she was spared that misfortune; she felt every thrill of it. The fire rushed up her spine; now lightnings flashed before her eyes in turn.

The fire that had been left in his balls, from that great rush of magnetism, caused them to press hard against his root; the burning sensation extended now to his cock itself, and it began gradually to swell. He convulsively pressed her white shoulders a little harder, though his lips did not move. Then, for the last time, the blaze started down her spine; it reached her womb, she noted that slow, but gradual expansion of his rod begin; her womb seemed to be consumed with fierce flames; then suddenly, nature offered a moment's respite she spent vigorously.

For a very short period this was a relief, then the stream of passion's electricity began once more to scorch her sanctuary. The perfume of the hottest animal the world knows, a vigorously passionate girl about to be fornicated, filled the nostrils of both, and urged them on.

A cry from the trembling lover; he clasped his hands on her shoulders; his cock suddenly quivered, wriggling, as it were, from side to side without his hips moving.

The mighty head swelled in the clasps of her torrid lips.

A great throb shook the tool from root to head; she cried out; he reassured her, but without moving a muscle.

Then another throb; with it, a little more swelling.

The swelling head, enwrapped by her womb lips, opened that holy of holies ever so little.

Then the third throb, big as the other two combined, was the climax.

She screamed aloud, when a blistering, stinging, mighty charge of seed was squirted through that small opening, into the very center of her quivering womb itself.

Another massive stroke quickly followed, then another; all throwing their load of passion upon the trembling interior of that lovely creature's sacredest place.

And with every hot charge thrown into that sanctuary, the tortured girl screamed again and again, until the strokes came faster, and she simply lay there, half fainting, and gasped and moaned and shuddered in her passionate ecstacy, while he kept pouring from his lusty loins his glorious charges of passion's offering.

There the panting beauty lay under him, gasping and moaning and sighing and moaning again, and sometimes crying out, as the caress of joy thrilled her beyond restraint, until her lovely nest had received to the fullest extent his tribute of manly strength to her sweet, fresh, young beauty.

And there they lay, for a long time, slowly re-

turning to earth, as handsome and ardent a couple
as a bed ever brought together.

We must leave to imagination the recital of
the second blissful contact of that evening, where
the amorous young beauty was thoroughly
stroked, and also taught the mysteries of ondu-
lation.

To say that that day was their only day of love,
would be far from the truth.

CUNTS

PRETTY young girls have nice tickly little cunts between their legs for ardent young men to put stiff pricks into. Let any young man see a young girl's pretty, hairy cunt, and watch how his prick will come up standing! If a girl will sit with her legs apart, and then pull her dresses up, uncovering the lovely soft white thighs and the delicious little hairy place between them, any young man's prick will come out and get hard and stiff, and eager to come close and touch the soft young cunt.

Think of all the pretty cunts between young girls' legs as they walk about the streets, or lie asleep at night, and of all the manly pricks covered up in trousers. What joy when one of the cunts and one of the pricks come together! In dancing, bodies held close together, prick and cunt near to each other. It is not strange that young women and young men learn to desire each other

and want to go from dancing to lie together somewhere—even if they do not say so!

What a pleasure to meet at a dance in the country some girl who knows the delights of fucking,
who will go gladly from the hot, noisy room,
where her desires have been aroused by the close-
ness of your body to hers, to some quiet, cool,
dark corner of the woods and there lie down and
open her receptive cunt to the thrusts of her
eager prick! It is a joy to find such a girl, press
your body to hers in the rhythm of a delightful
waltz, feel her arms tighten, and know that as you
touch her legs in the dance her cunt is beginning
to twitch and tingle. Hold her close and let her
feel the pushing and throbbing of your prick as it
begins to get stiff from feeling the warmth of
her body through the clothing. Then take her
outside and kiss her until she opens her mouth
and clings to you in the delirious kiss that means
surrender. After that, put your arms about her,
and walk up the road to the pitch-black grove.
She will know for what you are going there, and
will stop you on the way for more and more ardent kisses, holding you close and rubbing her
body against yours. In the darkness of the grove
she will let you feel her young breasts, firm under
your caressing hand, and will press against you

with her legs. She will stand with her back against a tree, and let you lean against her and kiss her more, and as you raise her dresses she will part her legs, so that your fingers will find her hot young cunt, moist and open. How she will tremble and thrill as your fingers play with that lovely, hairy organ! She may put her hand on you, and find your prick, all hard and stiff and throbbing, and take it out and put it between her legs, and even make you fuck her that way, leaning against a tree!

Or she may sink to the soft ground, drawing you down to her, and lie there with her legs far apart, her cunt ready and open, and take you with sucking kisses, gasping and shaking with desire, her whole body enjoying the delicious fucking you will give her. And through the darkness you will hear the soft sounds of other happy couples, not far off, all aroused by the dance, enjoying their fucking-play in the soft night.

But even in cities there are cunts that like to be fucked. If you know a full-blooded young woman, a young married woman who is keen, or a young widow who has not had a man for some time, take her out to a good dinner and after a few drinks drive her in your automobile to some quiet street in the suburbs and stop at some secluded spot away from the lights. Take her in your arms and kiss her, and she will be glad. If she is just drunk enough, or careless enough, and you are skilful, she will become so aroused with desire that she will let you take her to the back seat of your automobile and there give her the good fucking she longs for. Let your trousers down, sit there with your legs stretched out, and put her soft little hand on something big and hard. She will gasp and pull up her skirts and put herself astride of you, and let her quivering cunt come down for a delicious, satisfying fucking on your stiff prick.

Best is a discreet young widow or divorced woman, who has learned the delights of fucking and must indulge herself every few weeks. By waiting a month or so between times, she becomes so eager to feel a manly prick thrusting between her legs that she will not hesitate at all to let a suitable man know, by unmistakable signs, that she longs for a good fucking. Her cunt wants to be tickled and pushed and crowded by a nice thick prick, and if you are the man who meets with her favor at the time she will give you the opportunity to take her and fuck her to the delighted satisfaction of both of you.

One summer I met a young divorced woman,

who soon showed that she liked me. I used to call at her apartments for tea. We often kissed, and she kissed warmly, but I withheld myself, curious, to see what she would do. I knew that she desired me, and she knew that I desired her. One afternoon, after we had had our tea and a few highballs, and a few more than usually ardent kisses, she excused herself and left the room. After a few minutes she called to me. I found her in the half-opened door of her bedroom, clad only in a most delicious diaphanous pink nightdress, through which her beautiful body glowed blushing. No need for words; I carried her to the bed and there, naked in each other's arms, we enjoyed hours of the most delightful fucking, until both of us were quite exhausted.

There are so many pretty little cunts that ought to be fucked every now and then, and there are so few of them that get as much delicious fucking as they should have. Young girls mistakenly keep their cunts secreted and never use them, unless perhaps they finger them themselves, or let other girls finger them or rub them sometimes. Such innocent diversions are better than nothing, of course, but to enjoy all the pleasure their cunts can give them, girls ought to let themselves be fucked. Of course, there is danger in

promiscuous fucking—danger of horrible diseases
and danger of nameless children. But if a girl
is discreet, and careful to associate with clean
young men and see that proper precautions are
taken she can get a good, satisfying fucking now
and then with no danger at all.

A girl can easily show a young man what she
wants without being too bold, and if he is any
sort of a young fellow at all he will be more than
glad to give it to her. Think, girls, of the thrill
of knowing that "it" is going to happen to you!
You will be scared at first, when he comes to you,
but if he is a decent fellow he will soon love you,
and kiss you, and hold you close and play with
you, so that in a very short time you will be
kissing him back, and clinging to him, and want-
ing him to love you more. And you will not mind,
then, when he puts his hands on your legs. How
good it will feel to have his hands touching your
bare legs, coming closer and closer to your maiden
cunt! Let him finger you for a while and fondle
you there, and you will want him so much that
you will be glad and excited to see his long, hard
prick come out. Then lie back and surrender yourself to him; open your waist so that he may play
with your breasts; pull up your dresses, put your
legs apart, let him come in between them and put

106

his prick in your cunt—then close your eyes and feel the dear lad with your whole body, your first man, as he fucks you. As you lie there, with your body held tight in his arms, you will think "At last I am being fucked! I am a woman now, and a man is fucking me! His hard prick is actually in my cunt, and this delicious sensation which I feel as he pushes and thrusts is from his big, loving prick fucking my cunt."

Girls, after you have once been fucked by a nice, lovely boy with a big, thick prick, you will enjoy living, and nothing in the world will give you more satisfaction than letting your cunt be used now and then—not too often—for a sweet-delicious fucking.

I WANT A WOMAN

AM ALONE, a stranger in a strange city. I see women all around me, passing on the streets, but they are all strangers. Among them are painted faces and glances of invitation, but I do not want a whore, a drunken, diseased thing, I want a clean, wholesome, laughter-loving woman with a taste for a little adventure with a clean, wholesome man.

I am a clean, wholesome man! I have batted around a bit, but I have kept my self-respect and have had nothing to do with the filth of prostitutes. I have kept free from all their uncleanness and disease. But I have a man's appetite for a woman's body, and have loved from time to time many women who have felt free to love me and to take the pleasure I could give them by the freedom of their bodies to give me pleasure, too. I have found them charming women, too, and quite able to maintain their positions as ladies, yes, and as good wives and mothers, too, in some cases, while doing as they pleased in the matter of getting a little extra enjoyment out of life by a night or two with me now and then.

I have been months now without the sight of a woman except in public places. I have been continent too long—I want a woman all to myself, to play with, to have play with me, to enjoy, and to give pleasure to. I find myself lying awake at night thinking about the kind of a woman I should enjoy. I do not want a child, or a young girl, or a virgin. I do not like green fruit. I have heard of men who could enjoy nothing but virgins, but that always seemed to me a perverted taste. A young girl's maidenhood should be taken from her only under the most romantic circumstances, in the tender flush of young love. Otherwise she is spoiled forever. For a full-grown man to take maidenheads, captured or bought for the purpose, is gross brutality. I have taken but one in my life, and that was my wife's—and I do not recall that I, or she either, got much pleasure from the taking of it.

No, I want a woman whose virginity is gone; who is ripe for love, with enough experience to meet a man part way in the game. A woman about twenty-five (I am forty), a young wife or widow, or a bachelor maid who has not ruined her physical life by prizing virginity too highly;

preferably one who has not borne children, who has kept the firm breasts of the young childless woman.

Well, suppose I have her, how would I wish to take her? I'll tell you. Assuming that we have become acquainted to the point at which we begin to understand each other—at which she begins to feel that I desire more of her than just her company to dinners and dances and I begin to see that she is willing to give me more—assuming, then, that we understood each other, I would ask her to dine with me, and after making it quite clear (in a delicate way, of course) during our dinner that I was anxious to know her better, I would have her dance with me. In dancing it is possible for a man and woman to exchange certain confidences without saying a word. Being assured by certain little answering pressures when I pressed her a little closely in the dance that she was willing to go further, I would suggest a taxi drive, and in the taxi would try her out further by a few gentle caresses. If she permits my hand to clasp her leg above the knee, she will allow me to draw her to me and kiss her, and if she gives me back an open-mouthed kiss it only remains to set the date for a night of more intimate delights.

I have a very secluded little bungalow in which,

when the time comes, I bring her very discreetly after dark, in my own machine. She takes off her cloak, and I lead her into my living-room, where there is a cheerful log fire burning, with a great, comfortable couch in front of it. She is just a little excited, perhaps, and I bring cocktails. Now it is a fact that I like a woman just a little bit tipsy—not drunk, but with three or four drinks in her so that she is the least bit intoxicated. I usually find it easy to get them to that point— if they come with me at all, they will drink and enjoy it.

As we sit side by side drinking our cocktails— or high-balls—I allow myself some familiar caresses, with kisses. She answers readily to the kisses and soon responds warmly to the caresses. If she is just about drunk enough it will be fun now to put my hand in her bosom and feel her breasts—firm, well-rounded, delicious to the touch —and, kissing her ardently, I then unfasten her clothing so that her breasts are exposed. Wonderful things, a woman's breasts, round, soft, white with beautiful rosy nipples, warm, delicate! I love them more than any other part of a woman. I sometimes think that I could get entire satisfaction from a woman by the freedom of her breasts to my hands and lips. I confess, I have never tried it, as I have never had to stop there. In fact, if a man gets to the point of having a woman bare her breasts to him he will not be allowed to stop there!

There she lies, in a corner of my couch, in the firelight, her clothing disordered, her breasts in my hands, beneath my lips. I kiss them and nibble until she begins to stir with desire. Her hands caress my head, she lies back with her eyes closed, little tremors go through her, and she begins to murmur terms of endearment. I can now assure her that I love her, and I do so, in ardent terms, moulding her breasts with my hands and covering her lips with kisses. She returns the kisses with wet, outturned lips against mine, her hands hold my hands and press them against her breasts, and she returns my words of love.

Still crowded against her as she lies back the pillows in the corner of the couch, I put my hand beneath her skirts. I clasp her calf, her knees; I stroke and fondle her leg higher, higher, and if her drawers are of the lacy, open kind, I soon have my hand on her naked thigh. Continuing to kiss her madly, and press against her, I fondle and caress the warm, soft skin, up her thigh to her hip, then across her abdomen until my fingers reach the soft, curly hair that grows there. Tick-

113

ling and lightly touching the soft curls my fingers proceed gradually, gently, down between her legs, and touch and tickle there until of her own accord she parts her legs a little and lets my whole hand find and clasp what is between them.

After a few minutes' delicious play of fingers there, during which she lies quite passive, except for the uninterrupted sucking of her kisses and an occasional pressure of her hands, I begin with one hand to undo my clothing. As soon as she sees my purpose, she begins to loosen hers. I leave her now; her adoring eyes follow me as I mix another drink and bring it to her. This is a stiff one, but she drinks it off thirstily. Then I draw her to her feet and whisper to her that I want her naked. I lead her to a screened corner, and returning to the couch lay off my own clothes and sit down to wait.

LOVE'S ENCYCLOPAEDIA

Part I

INTRODUCTION

Necessity for the Book.—History of Fucking.

HILE there are numerous books and pamphlets issued on sexual intercourse, or "fucking" as it is generally known, they are mostly in the form of stories, and there is no single book published that contains complete information or advice on this particular question. Every other science has its text books and its lecturers, but the art of fucking is neglected. Fucking is an art. The mere fact of introducing the cock in the cunt and moving it in and out until the ejaculation of spunk is not art. True, it is fucking, but the difference between that way of doing it and the way it should be done, is like the difference between a child's first drawing and a picture by the world's greatest painter. Therefore, this book is necessary, and if followed closely by any couple, will enable them to enjoy sexual pleasures they had not even dreamed possible before. This book is a complete manual on sexual indulgence between man and woman. It is a well-known fact, that after a young couple are married and have fucked for a month or so, they begin to look around for some way to vary the pleasure, and they try to discover for themselves the different positions possible in fucking. These attempts are, for the most part, clumsy, but they show the craving that nature demands to be satisfied, and it is often years before they learn the little tricks and secrets that increase their health and pleasure.

Nature intends men and women to fuck. Everything in nature fucks. The flowers, birds, insects and animals all have sexual intercourse. Fucking dates back to Adam and Eve, and can be plainly traced down to date. The old Hebrew tribes were great fuckers, the men being blessed with great vitality. Ten and twelve wives for each man was a common thing, and it was not counted strange for one of these old time men to fuck the whole dozen, one after the other. There was no attempt to prevent conception. Civilization had not progressed so far, and the women had babies, one each year. As the human race grew older it began to look around for means to prevent conception, with the result that "withdrawing" was hit upon, which still remains the most popular method of all. With the discovery of the prevention of conception, the number of women to a man grew less and less, for it was not necessary to stop fucking while the woman was bearing children.

The age to begin fucking has always been a question much discussed, but eminent doctors now agree that there should be no age set, each person following the dictates of nature in that regard. Some boys and girls begin to feel this call as early as eight years, while others not until sixteen or seventeen. Boys particularly begin to get the craving when the stuff begins to descent to their balls, and in some countries, notably Persia, France, etc. it is a common practice for the women to watch these young boys carefully and to suck off and swallow the first seminal fluid that enters their balls, this first emission being highly beneficial to the women's health and complexion. Some mothers of young boys even arrange for having them sucked for a year after the stuff first appears, before they are allowed sexual intercourse, the sucking strengthening and developing their sexual powers and laying the foundation for a strong vitality in after years.

It is hoped that a careful perusal of the following pages and strict attention to the methods, etc. laid down, will show the way for many couples to complete sexual enjoyment, and this book is dedicated to all couples who seek the true art of fucking.

LOVE'S ENCYCLOPEDIA

CHAPTER I

Sexual Organs of Man and Woman

Although meant for each other, men and women are constructed in an entirely different manner, especially regarding their genative organs, which particularly distinguish one sex from the other. These organs are placed at the bottom of the belly, between the thighs.

The sexual organs of the male are composed of a canal covered with flesh and muscle, forming their mass a member more or less long and thick and round, springing from a kind of bag of skin containing two reservoirs, shaped like beans, also more or less large. This canal is called the urethra, and the entire organ is known as prick, cock, and hundred other significant names such as lance, dagger, tool, spear, dart, etc. The prick grows out of the lower part of the belly between the man's legs at a spot called the "pubis" which becomes covered with hair at the age of puberity,

119

which is when the stuff begins to flow into his
balls for the first time. The end of the prick
terminates in a kind of an acorn, split at the end,
which is covered with a movable skin which folds
back at will and during fucking, so as to leave
the head naked and render the tickling of the
sexual parts, of the woman greater when introduced therein. This head, when the foreskin is
drawn back, is covered with a membrane closely
resembling the skin of the lips. This movable
skin is called the "foreskin" and is fastened to
the lower part of the head or acorn by a kind of
membrane on one side called the fraenum, which
gets partly ruptured at the first fuck of the man
to permit the foreskin to move backward. This
membrane is very delicate and to stretch it by
pulling the foreskin strongly back gives the man
great pleasure. The seat of pleasure is this sensitive top of his prick, and by caressing it and tickling it you are sure to bring about the emission
of his seed, spunk, or stuff as it is generally called.
This stuff is a whitish, semi-fluidous liquid with a
slightly bitter taste, which when spurted into the
sexual part of woman, operates to fecundate the
female. By this organ the man also pisses. The
bag underneath the prick is nothing more than
the prolongation of the skin of the prick and

the insides of the thighs, and this also gets hairy at the age of puberty. This bag contains the two reservoirs mentioned above. These reservoirs are glandular organs about the size of walnuts, and secrete the spunk or stuff of the male. They are called testicles or balls. The whole organ of the male swells up and stands out when the man has fucking desires or when nature wishes that the stuff in his balls should be voided. It becomes stiff and hard resembling a broom handle and reaches a size from about four inches to eight inches ordinarily, although some men have pricks 12 inches long, and some African savages have pricks as thick as an arm and about 15 inches long. This stiffening is called an erection, or getting a "hard on", a "cock stand", etc.

The woman's sexual parts are composed of a slit, which is called "vulva" from the Latin, meaning a doorway. This slit begins at the bottom of the belly at the pubis, which, as in the male becomes covered with hair at the time of puberty or when the menses commence. This slit terminates near the arse hole. Lifting open the two large outer lips we find therein two little tongues or lips, at the summit of which, the point where they meet at top, is a kind of a little button or growth of flesh, resembling the top of a man's prick, only a good deal smaller. This is called clitoris, button, etc., and is the sexual enjoyment in the woman, exactly as the head of the male's prick is for the man. Beneath this clitoris is a small hole through which the woman pisses, and the beneath this small hole is a larger hole with elastic ridges which is the entrance to the passage in the woman's body called the vagina. This vagina extends inward about 7 or 8 inches to the neck to the woman's womb, which is the name given to the place in the woman's body where children are conceived and nourished previous to birth. This vagina opening is partially stopped up, when the woman is a virgin, by a thin membrane called the "hymen". The slit of the woman and all the organs together is called the cunt", and has many figurative names such as "pussy", "sheath", "birds-nest", "cave of love", etc. The female stuff has no prolific value in conception, but its emission causes indescribable enjoyment to the woman, and is of great benefit to the male as it is absorbed into his system when his prick is in the woman's cunt. Besides the parts above, the female has on her chest two halfmoons which develop about the age of puberty and become more or less large with age, filling with milk when the woman is a mother. These demiglobes vary in size and shape, being sometimes close together and sometimes wide apart. Each of them has in the middle a little pink. button called nipple These nipples stand up hard during sexual enjoyment. The two globes are known as bubbies, breasts, titties and charms, this latter word being used to describe all organs of the woman also.

Fucking is the introduction of the manly prick into the female cunt, and the action of the couple in moving it in and out until the spunk of the male is spurted into the woman's vagina.

The woman, however, is often termed "cunt all over" and the contact of any part of her pleases and excites the man, and her whole body invites the burning spunk of the male. The benefit of this is described in another chapter.

CHAPTER II

The Five Different Methods of Fucking Described

There are, broadly speaking, five different and distinct methods for a man and woman to enjoy the pleasures of love. First: Ordinary Fucking; Second: Bottom or Arse Fucking; Third: French Fucking or Sucking; Fourth: Hand Fucking or Frigging and Fifth: Body Fucking. Absolutely every way that a man and woman together can "fuck" comes under the head of one of these methods, and to be able to say that they are true disciples of love, no man or woman should slight or neglect any one of these methods. We will take up, in the order given, each of the five methods named, and describe them carefully.

A general rule applies to those wishing to enjoy themselves fully. All intercourse should occur in a cozy, secret nook, safe from surprises and prying eyes. There should be a soft carpet or rug, a good spring bed (not too soft) a low couch or sofa, an arm-chair and ordinary chairs and

125

plenty of pillows and cushions. There should, if possible, be running water in the room, plenty of towels, several sponges, some perfume, and something to eat and drink. Last of all, the man and woman should strip absolutely naked, for that is the only costume suitable for true fuckers.

The Ordinary

The woman lies on her back, on a bed or anywhere else. She opens her legs and thighs, and receives between them her lover, who kneels between the knees of the girl. The man then leans over, supporting himself on his hands near the woman's shoulders. They are now belly to belly. The woman now reaches down and taking the man's stiff standing prick in her hand places it at the entrance of her cunt. The man then stretches out to full length on the woman, pushing his prick into her cunt at the same time, until his chest rests upon her breasts. The woman than throws her arms around the man's neck and also places her legs and thighs over his loins. The couple then push up and down slowly and steadily, the man's cock slipping in and out of the woman's cunt, until the spermatic outbreak, the woman shooting first, if possible, and the man last, if not possible for them to shoot together. At the ap-

126

proach of the sensation which precedes the seminal spurting, the couple should fuck violently until the stuff spurts, when the man should bury himself as far as possible in the woman and not remove his prick until every drop of sperm has been voided from his balls. This latter remark will apply to all sexual intercourse no matter how done, subject however to the remarks contained in Chapter 5 relating to the prevention of conception.

Bottom or Arse Fucking

The woman kneels on the bed on her hands and knees, her arse standing out, the man back of her, which brings his prick on the level with the woman's arse, into which he inserts it. Leaning over the woman's back a little he should pass one hand around her body and while fucking her bum should tickle and rub her cunt, and with the other hand rub and press her bubbies, tickling the little pink nipples at the same time. Until the woman's arse hole is sufficiently large to admit the man's prick, it should be thoroughly saturated with olive oil or vaseline. The head of the man's prick should always be also thoroughly annointed with vaseline. The entrance should never be made by violence, but with great care, and more than two inches of prick should never be inserted. There are numerous couples who have never experienced the pleasures of arse fucking, who are afraid that the large male member would hurt in entering their arse holes. By using the precautions mentioned above, an entrance can easily be accomplished, although it may take three or four connections before the woman's hole is open enough to permit the easy insertion of the. prick. No matter how large this hole becomes the man's prick should be annointed previous to entrance to make the pleasure greater.

French Fucking

This is the name given to the method of intercourse obtained by the sucking of the cock and cunt by the man and woman, and derives its name from the fact that it is the univesal practice of French men and women. The original way of sucking is known as "69" from the fact that these two numbers represent the position of the couple while doing it. There are several variations of positions in this, as well as in every other one of the five methods. These variations are described in Chapter 7.

The woman lies on her back in bed, her thighs open and her knees uplifted. The man straddles over her facing her feet on his knees, the woman's head being between his thighs. He then stretches out to his full length supporting himself on his elbows which come at the side of her hips, his face being hidden between her thighs. Passing his hands under her arse he gently opens the lips of her cunt and places his mouth upon it, frisking his stiffened tongue all around the woman's clitoris. He must also plunge his tongue as far into the interior of her cunt as he can, sucking the clitoris and drawing it up into his mouth, being careful that his teeth do not come into contact with it and hurt the woman. During this time the woman should with one hand place his stiff prick in her mouth, nibbling and sucking it, tickling the fraenum and ruby head with her tongue, holding the foreskin tightly back. With the other hand she should tickle, caress, press and dangle the man's balls, the root of the prick not entirely in her mouth, and last but not least his bottom hole. This should be continued until the approach of the essence of love, when the woman should suck madly at the throbbing prick as if trying to get it all down her mouth, and the man at the same time should return the pleasure by doing the same to his partner, drawing the clitoris into his mouth while pulling at the entire cunt with all his power. Thus each receives into the mouth the spunk of the other without quitting their post until the discharge is complete and the reservoirs dry, either swallowing or rejecting afterwards, the divine liquid so voluptuously emitted.

Frigging

Frigging is the manipulation by the hands of a man and woman upon each other's sexual organs, and is one of the most popular sexual sports, being used largely in places more or less public where any other method of sexual enjoyment would be too conspicuous. It is one of the most delightful forms of sex enjoyments, which explains in universal use. The proper way is as follows, although there is no end of positions a couple can take, as long as they are able to reach each other's genitals with one or both hands. The man as well as the woman are seated on the edge of the bed, couch, bench, or in fact anywhere. The man should be seated on the right side of the woman. He puts his left hand around her waist and mauls her bubbies, or under her arse to press her bottom. With his right hand he gently opens the lips of the woman's cunt and tickles her clitoris with one finger, pushing it in and out and around in every direction. He should also moisten his thumb and index finger, and

130

pressing his thumb on the clitoris, insert his index finger into the woman's vagina. Then rapidly and lightly he moves his fingers thus placed backwards and forwards first gently and then faster until the discharge appears. The man's nails should be cut short and well filled with wax, all jagged edges being carefully smoothed in order not to injure the delicate lining of the woman's vagina. A finger of a kid glove is often placed on the man's index finger with good effect.

The woman on her part takes her lover's stiff standing prick in her right hand and shakes it softly and voluptuously. She uncovers the sensitive head by drawing down the foreskin and pulling it up again, gently at first and then quicker, tightening her grasp so as to stretch the fraenum by drawing down the skin towards the root. During this time her left hand should press her lover's balls with a soft grasp, caressing the bag and its contents. She can also moisten her thumb and gently rub the ruby head of the throbbing prick as she is shaking it with her right hand, but the man's balls should be in her left hand when she shoots. All during this combat the couple should kiss, and press against each other until with many tender sighs they spurt their burning spunk into each other's hand, continuing their mutual manipulating until all the sperm is out of their respective organs. It will be seen in putting this method in practice that it is possible to fuck faster and more furiously than under any other method, no matter how young or vigorous the couple may be. In fact the object of frigging is to begin gently at first and work up to a furious pace, until at the final emission the man's spunk is spurted violently to a great height and the woman gushes a generous quantity into her lover's hands, both experiencing the highest possible form of sexual feeling.

Body Fucking

This way is really for the men alone, for the male is the only one who can get pleasure out of this method. However Chapter VII describes various combinations of body fucking with sucking and frigging, in which the woman joins, gaining as much pleasure as the man. However we give here the original method of body fucking.

The woman lies on her side on the bed; the man along side also, her bum being pressed up against his belly. The man then slips his prick between her thighs, close up to her cunt, and fucks her between her snowy columns as if he were in her cunt or arse hole. To heighten the illusion he plays with and feels all her charms, her bubbies and cunt, and she, twisting her head around towards him, gives him her mouth to kiss, while she tightens her thighs moving them gently together to excite by the touch of her smooth skin the emprisoned prick which rubs against the hair of her cunt while her white, round arse warms the man's belly. The woman can wet a finger and tickle and rub the ruby head as it appears from time to time at each thrust on his part between her legs. Such a combination soon forces his sluice gates to open, and quickly the woman feels his hot sperm bursting from his prick between her legs. This position is recommended for men wishing to fuck very young girls who are too small for an actual penetration of a prick, and should be used in this case in connection with sucking and frigging.

While the above descriptions give the five original methods of sexual intercourse, there are numerous variations which add to the zest and pleasure of the act. These are described in Chapter VII. There is but one rule to follow in doing the above, and is that no true loving couple can well afford to slight any one of the above methods, and should use all with equal frequency.

CHAPTER III

Why Fucking Is Necessary.—Fucking and Health. Fucking and Beauty

A few moments serious consideration on the subject of sexual intercourse will convince anyone of its absolute necessity to the welfare of the human race. Fucking is a part of nature, and is designed not only to increase the population, but for the complete development of man. Everything in nature fucks one way or the other. The male sperm of flowers is blown by the wind to the ovaries of female flowers, resulting in seed for a new flower. Insects, bugs, birds, fish, all animals have sexual intercourse. Civilization has developed the mind of man, and the mind has developed the art of intercourse to its present high state of perfection. No part of the human body is of any less importance than the other, consequently it is right for man to seek to develop his sexual powers in proportion to the progress he makes in developing his other powers.

135

Fucking is healthful. No single organ has more effect upon the human system than the organ of generation. We are strong or weak in ratio to the strength of these organs. Look at any perfect specimen of manhood or womanhood, and you will find that their sexual capacity is practically unlimited; of course, everyone cannot be perfect, but by more careful attention to these parts, life can be made happier and more pleasurable than if no care or attention is paid to these priceless organs ,which nature has given you. The benefit of fucking is no better illustrated than by watching any newly married couple. Beginning a few weeks after marriage, it is noticed that the man is becoming stouter and better looking, with the flush of health upon his cheeks. His step is lighter and his eyes shine with the light of determination. The woman at the same time begins to change. Her breasts begin to fill out and her bottom becomes rounder, while her whole body takes on a more dignified air. Everyone knows that a young couple just married are continually fucking, but even though inclined to do so to excess, they perform the act regularly, which is the secret of good health. This continues for a varying number of months, but all "roast beef" at a feast in time loses its piquancy. This is where the science of fucking should be applied. Those who utilize the five methods outlined in Chapter II lose none of the zest of the act; in fact they are tremendously strengthened and are able to fuck during their whole married life with as much pleasure as though still on their honey-moon.

It is a well known fact that the male sperm or stuff has certain medical and healthful properties. Famous singers have found that the best way to keep their marvelous voices fresh and clear was by sucking a man's prick, the hot stuff spurting through their vocal cords strengthening them and making the voice softer and richer. At the same time the exercise of sucking brings into play certain muscles of the neck and throat that are otherwise slight, and the sperm whitens the teeth. Many women vary the swallowing of the stuff by pulling the prick from their mouths at the critical moment, receiving the essence of love spurting on their faces, neck or busts. This makes the skin soft and white, removes freckles and blackheads and keeps them from having a sallow or muddy complexion. There are hundreds of women, whose soft white hands are the envy of their friends, and who attribute the fact to the practice of frigging and allowing the stuff to bathe their hands. The woman's stuff is as beneficial to the man for the same reason. The French people have the reputation of being the handsomest of any, their complexion being kept in condition by means of sucking, and from which fact the term "French funck" is obtained. There is practically no taste to the sperm of the man and woman, aside from a slight salty one. It is not unpleasant. On the contrary, it is agreeable or sucking would not be in such favor. It is not necessary for the woman to swallow the stuff to gain its benefits, although the benefits are quicker when swallowed. The mere fact of the prick being in her mouth gives her great benefit. A five minute suck each day, even without bringing on the man's emission, will do wonders with the complexion and throat. A favorite method is to preceed each fuck with a short suck.

CHAPTER IV

How to Seduce Girls, Young Girls and Married Women

How Women and Girls Seduce Boys

Women are queer creatures, and are particularly strange in sexual matters. To the man who makes up his mind to fuck a certain woman, however, there is no such word as fail, and there is no reason why he should not be successful provided he goes at the matter in a careful, systematic way.

We will take first ordinary girl of from 16 years old and upwards. From 16 to about 25 she is a curious creature and very anxious to absorb knowledge of sexual facts. As long as parents persist in keeping children ignorant of fucking, just so long will it be easier for men to seduce girls, for it is only natural that they should seek to know the meaning of the fires that are burning in them.

The first thing a man must do is to become well

139

acquainted with the object of his endeavor. This
he can do by taking her to various places of
amusement, etc. After a few weeks of this (the
time can best be judged by the man himself),
he should begin to take little liberties. If they
are sitting side by side in a secluded spot, he
could rest his hand unconsciously upon her knee
while talking, and place his arm around her. If
she will permit him to kiss her at this time, so
much the better, but the true pursuer never
rushes things, for the pleasure to be experienced
from fucking a virgin, more than compensates for
the delay. A girl is excited by bodily contact.
The more the man can get her to lean against
him the better, and he should also lean on her,
if possible over her in the position preliminary
to fucking. Numerous kisses and hugs will work
a girl up to fever heat, and by kissing her in
her mouth and tickling her tongue with yours,
he excites her sexual instinct more than anything
else. He should also mould her bubbies, and if
she permits that his hand should go under her
clothes. If this should cause her any uneasiness, laugh it off and kiss her. She will probably
be in such a heat that she will let it pass. Then
place your hand up further until it reaches her
cunt. If she objects, tell her it will not harm her.

Most girls will not permit the prick to be inserted, but are afraid of the consequences. It is then up to the man to convince the girl that there is such a thing as fucking without getting babies. He should describe the pleasure of the act to her. He should beg to be permitted to show her how it is done without doing it. She will probably let him do this and he should press his prick to her cunt in the fucking position, kissing her with the tongue at the same time. This will probably be all that is necessary, for the girl will do the rest, shoving her arse around until the prick begins to slide in. A man who succeeds in fucking a girl this way should use every precaution to keep her from getting in the family way by withdrawing his prick at the first approach of the final seminal spasm, and shooting outside. He owes this to the girl.

Another way to obtain the object is for the man to become acquainted with the girl as before, and after taking her out several times, propose a little supper party with some friends. He must then hire a private dining room with a door that can be locked, and bribe the waiter. At the appointed time he can take the girl here, and after waiting for the friends (who of course will not show up, not being invited) proceed to dine alone

with her. He should see that she drinks plenty
of wine, it being a good idea to have some strong
whiskey mixed with whatever drink she takes to
hasten the result. It won't be long before she is
a little wobbly. The man must then see that the
door is locked. He now has the girl at his mercy,
but he should get her passions aroused the same
as explained previously before fucking her,
though it will not take as long, and should she
object he can then enforce his point better by
proceeding to fuck her anyway. She will probably make no great objection, being under the influence of drinks, and it will be an easy matter
to get the prick into the cave of love it has been
waiting and longing to enter.

The fucking of girls under 16 years of age is
a different matter, especially with those who have
never had their Monthlies. Many men prefer
these youngsters to the older ones, on account
of their freshness. Young girls will permit more
liberties than older ones, but the man must first
become very thoroughly in their confidence. It
is then an easy matter to get them to go to a
room you must have engaged, and a few glasses
of champaign will work wonders. They are very
eager to know sexual facts, and you should talk
along those lines, showing them pictures of men

and women fucking and sucking. Allow them to examine your prick, and suck them to show how it feels. It is then an easy matter to get them to suck you which they will do to the queen's taste. Unless the girl is well developed a man should not attempt to fuck her in the ordinary way, but rather employ her to suck him. However, these youngsters make good fucking, but the entrance should never be made by violence, and plenty of vaseline should be used to help the insertion.

Married women are less difficult to get to fuck than any others, on account of the fact that they have no fears of losing a maidenhead, and generally know how to avoid having babies. However, the only married women who fuck with other men are those dissatisfied with their own partners, and the man should look for these only. Young wives of old husbands are good hunting grounds, or wives who go out all the time without their husbands. A little attention to these women is often appreciated, although care should be taken that the husband is not aware of it, and it is an easy matter to suggest fucking to them on account of their knowledge of it. The pleasure is greater, too, for "stolen fruit is the sweetest".

Women are not the only persons seduced. Many

girls and women seduce young boys up to twelve
years of age (older ones not needing any seduc-
tion) and use them to good advantage. A young
boy is generally not as particular about exposing
his privates as a girl is, and it is only a matter
of the woman getting him in a room alone with
her. She should be in a nightgown and get the
boy to come to bed with her. A good way to begin is to play the game of "touch". The object of
this game is for the girl and to pull the covers
over them, and touch each other on different
parts of the body without the other stopping
them. The boy's efforts will be directed to almost
any part of the woman's body of course, but the
woman should gradually lead toward his prick.
This game will become very exciting, during which
the covers will fall from them. The woman then
should promise to show the boy something, if he
won't tell. This probably will have its effect, and
the boy will promise. She would then suck his
prick. It will get stiff and hard although very
thin and not very long. It is an easy matter to
get him to fuck her then, she putting the youth
on top of her. If the boy's stuff has not yet descended to his balls he will maintain an erection as
long as the woman desires, while she can shoot to
her heart's content. It is an easy matter to train

144

the boy to suck her after a beginning is once made, and many happy hours can be spent in this delicious pastime, the woman sucking the boy at the same time.

LOVE'S ENCYCLOPAEDIA

Part II

CHAPTER V

The Best Method of Preventing Conception

Now we come to the most important Chapter in the book, "The Prevention of Conception". There are thousands upon thousands of women who never fully enjoy fucking on account of the fear of "getting caught", resulting in the dreaded swelling behind the navel which rarely goes down under nine months. There is no reason in the world why the prevention of conception should not be more fully known. If we were given our sexual organs merely for the purposes of creating babies, our men and women would have to be contented with but one connection every year, presuming that each time they fucked, a child was the result. No sane person can agree that fucking is meant for this one purpose. Our sexual organs were given us to use, they are as much a part of our systems as our hearts, stomachs, etc. Consequently there must be some means to prevent conception, and the following methods are given and recommended as harmless and efficient Abortion is a crime and works untold misery on the health of the woman who practices it. It is not necessary, for with proper precautions, there is no danger of getting in the family way. The pleasures of fucking more than compensate the partners for any little inconvenience they may undergo to prevent conception, and the person who is either too careless or lazy to take precautions either should not fuck or else should be satisfied with having one baby every eleven or twelve months.

The principle of conception is simple and should be understood by everyone. Once each month, in a woman, a minute egg or ovum descends upon her ovaries into her womb. This is accomplished by a flow of blood called "menses" or "monthlies". This egg remains in the womb for an indefinite period; in some women it passes off, or is dried up, in a week and in some not until fifteen or twenty days. If during the time this egg is in the woman's womb she is fucked and some of the man's sperm (no matter how small the quantity) succeeds in entering her womb, she is "caught" and a new being is started by the action of his sperm upon her egg. It is not necessary for her to "come" or "shoot" during the connection. She can even be unconscious and get caught.

From this it is seen that by keeping the sperm from entering the woman's womb, conception cannot take place. Consequently by fucking the "French Way" (sucking) by "Frigging" or by any of the "Body Fucking" methods, the man's prick does not enter the woman's cunt at all and there is no opportunity for the sperm to enter her womb. "Bottom Fucking" can also be indulged in without danger.

However, for those who do not wish to confine themselves to any of the above methods, the following means of preventing conception are given.

Withdrawing

The easiest and simplest means of keeping from having babies, and a method which has been used ever since the world began is called "Withdrawing". The name is self explanatory and I doubt whether there is a single married couple in the entire universe who have not used this method time and time again. The man should continue to pull in and out slowly until he feels the approach of the vital fluid. He should not wait until the first spurt of the hot stuff, but should pull out when he begins feeling the symptome of its approach. If the man is fucking in the usual position, that is, lying on the woman, the woman underneath, he should raise himself from her on his arms, so that only their stomachs are connected. In this position it is clear for her to grab it in her hand, and after pulling out to shove his prick in a position over the woman's stomach. This leaves it clear for her to grab it in her hand and continue the pleasure for the man by frigging him until the stuff spurts, receiving the liquid in her palm, on her stomach or breasts or where ever it might go. This not only intensifies the pleasure to the woman, for a normal woman is glad to feel her lover's sperm upon her body, and takes pleasure in making him shoot as large a quantity as he can by gently squeezing his balls while frigging his prick, the squeezing making him spurt an enormous amount and to a greater distance than ordinarily. An enjoyable way to practice withdrawing is for the woman to get on top while fucking, and the man underneath. At the approach of the stuff, the man tells the woman, and she pulls her arse backwards, which makes his prick slip out. Sliding down about six inches, she again lays flat upon him, breast to breast. The man's prick is now tightly pressed between his and his partner's stomach, where they continue their movements until the stuff spurts out. In this position the pleasure is greater by feeling the sticky stuff moistening their bodies.

The Syringe

Under this method the fuckers enjoy themselves to their heart's content in any position, until the man shoots. Then, without a moment's delay, the woman must jump up and syringe herself out. In doing this a fountain syringe is best. This should be filled before the couple go into action with cold water, to which has been added a solution of two table spoons of powdered borax in a cup of cold water, dissolved. Three drops of carbolic acid can be substituted for the borax if desired; or two tablespoons of vinegar can also be utilized. In this method, while shooting, the man should lay perfectly still, at the same time drawing his prick about half of its length. By doing this there is less chance of the stuff spurting into the woman's womb before she can syringe it out of her. Be sure that the woman gets up immediately, for the success of this method lies in syringing the man's stuff out before it reaches the womb.

Condoms

A condom is a thin india-rubber tube, closed at one end, the exact size and shape of a male prick. They are to be placed on the prick immediately before fucking, and serve to keep the man's sperm in this covering at the critical moment. They are so thin that they interfere but little with the man's pleasure and none at all with the woman's. They are for sale by nearly all drug stores, and cost from $2. to $5. per dozen, or 25 to 50 cents each. They should be blown up before using to guard against any pin holes which would allow the stuff to enter the woman while shooting, for unless this is done, their use is a delusion and a snare. It is wise to remove them at once after intercourse and blow them up with the stuff together to see whether a hole has been worked in them during fucking. However, there is small danger of this, provided the couple take things easy and do not fuck furiously. They should be washed in cold water within a short time after using, carefully dried, and dusted with talcum powder. As the man's prick in this method does not touch any part of the girl, to make a perfect fuck she should suck him previous to his pulling the condom on, but not enough to make him shoot.

This will moisten his prick and render the act more enjoyable to him.

Intervals

Bearing in mind the principal of conception, how the egg in the female passes from her or is dried up and worthless after a certain number of days from her "monthlies", it is a scientific and medical truth that if she be fucked between the time this egg is worthless and up to a few days previous to her next monthlies, she cannot get in the family way. Consequently the couple can fuck without any precautions whatever during this time without danger. However, as the time varies with each girl, the method is not absolutely safe, but the average time the egg is worthless in the girl is twelve days after her monthlies, and up to five days previous to her next. The only way to be sure of the exact time of a particular girl is by experimenting, but as such experimenting would probably result in several babies, it is better to use some other means of prevention.

Sponges

These are made, expressly for the purposes of prevention of conception, 'sanitary sponges". These are small silk sponges, the size of a walnut, to which are attached silken strings. These sponges should be soaked in a weak solution of vinegar and water and inserted by the woman up her vagina immediately previous to intercourse, the string being left outside. As to be of any effect, the male sperm must be pure and unadulterated when entering the womb, the purpose of the sponge is to catch the spurted stuff, and to render any that might get past it worthless by mixing it with the acid of the vinegar. These sponges can be made by any one. All that is necessary is to purchase a small silk sponge at any drug store, cut it to the size desired, sew two or three silk threads securely to it, and it is ready for use. It is needless to say that they should be thoroughly cleaned after using.

Pessaries

In almost any drug stores can be purchased a soft rubber pessary, which is a rubber cap, designed to clasp over the neck of the womb. By the use of a pessary, a couple can fuck at will, knowing that no matter how often the man may shoot, the pessary will prevent any of the stuff from entering the girl's womb. These pessaries are removed a few days previous to the monthlies, and put in place a day or so after. Their use is not universal on account of the difficulty in placing them on the womb, very few women knowing exactly how to tell when the mouth of the womb is found. However, society people, actresses and those who are acquainted with some friendly doctor who will do the job use them exclusively. The pessaries cost anywhere from $2. to $4. each and last years.

Turned Womb

This is a physical prevention of conception. If a girl's womb is out of place, so that the neck or mouth instead of being in the vagina is pressing to either side or has fallen to the back, conception is not possible, for the womb, in turning, doubles on itself and prevents anything from entering it. Consequently the man's stuff cannot penetrate either, and no precautions are necessary. Although a girl with a turned womb suffers cramps during this pain than to be obliged to have babies.

CHAPTER VI

The Wedding Night. How to Prepare For It and How to Fuck the First Time.

Restoring Virginity.

More disappointment is experienced by young people on their wedding night than almost any other time. It is a common thing for a woman and man to approach this time of the first fuck without the least possible preparation, and consequently they are at a loss to explain the reason for their disappointment in not finding the first fuck as delightful as anticipated. To a girl, the first fuck is generally something she looks forward to with a certain dread, although her whole body and being is crying out for it. To the ordinary mind, the first fuck suggests violence in breaking the maidenhead and the girl generally shrinks from this pain. However, the first fuck can be made to give even more pleasure than any other by a couple who are in entire sympathy with each other. If done right, the slight pain

ccompanying the breaking of the girl's maiden-
ead will only make the bliss greater, provided
he man takes the precautions to work her pas-
ions up to fever heat, which the majority of
ewly wedded men do not think necessary.

It would be well on the girl's parts, for a week
previous to her wedding night, to bath her cunt,
and especially her maidenhead and the parts adjacent thereto with olive oil or melted vaseline,
repeating this operation every day. This will sof-
ten the membrane and render its breaking an
easy matter. No wise man will fuck a girl the
first time without preliminary steps to excite her.
After undressing, and getting in bed, it is an easy
matter to arouse passion through the medium of
kissing, hugging and feeling the kisses being especially given with the man's tongue inside the
woman's mouth tickling her tongue. His hand
should rub her breasts, tickling the nipples, and
should wander down to her cunt caressing the
button with his finger. A few minutes of this
will make the girl anxious for the real thing. The
man should then get up and anoint his stiff prick
with a liberal supply of vaseline. Do not be stingy
with it, but put it on thick. All that is necessary to be so lubricated is the head of the prick,
the foreskin being pulled back and the vaseline

applied directly to the naked head. A dab of vaseline on the girl's cunt at the entrance to her vagina will be of help also. The first fuck should always be done in the position described in Chapter II under heading "Ordinary" as the various positions described in Chapter VII can only be done after the woman's cunt is open enough to receive the man's prick easily. During this first fuck the woman should continue to hold the man's prick, guiding it in, and the man should not attempt to break the maidenhead by one mighty thrust, as that will tear the delicate skin surrounding it and make the girl too sore. With her guiding his stiff tool in they should gently move their asses in uniform motion, the man going in no further than the girl will allow him. By this method the prick slips easily into place, the breaking of the maidenhead only increasing the pleasure of the girl. The man should not seek to bury his prick to the balls in the woman the first time, as it will take two or more fucks before the prick will be able to unfold the closed vagina and open the canal.

The advantages of taking time to do first fucking properly is this. If the entrance is made through violence, and the maidenhead broken and the entire canal opened at one thrust of the prick, the pain to the woman will be always remembered to the man's discredit while at the same time the action will injure the delicate muscles of the mouth and length of the vagina. Consequently the woman's hole becomes large, and before long, the muscles not being there to react, the man's prick will fit loosely therein. On the other hand, if care is taken at the first intercourse, the muscles always remain firm, and all subsequent fucks are greatly enhanced by the muscles of woman's vagina holding the man's inserted prick in a tight, throbbing embrace, during the entire screw.

It is not a bad idea for couples engaged to be married to come to a full understanding regarding their sexual life previous to marriage, and a book like this can be read by them together and followed to great advantage.

If a girl has been fucked before marriage and does not want her husband to know it, she can stimulate virginity and completely deceive the man by syringing herself with a strong solution of alum and water, beginning several days previous to the wedding day. This will pucker her cunt up tight and render it hard to insert the prick. She should, while being fucked the wedding night hold herself tightly together to render it more difficult for the man to enter, and at the same time complain of the pain, acting as nearly as she can remember, the same as the time she lost her maidenhead.

CHAPTER VII

Thirty-two Variations in Fucking Described.

Variety is the spice of life. This is true in all human relationship, but more particularly in the sexual connection, and no man or woman can say they have got the best out of fucking until they have done the act in all its various positions. In this chapter we give all the principal variations, but these can be increased one hundred per cent by any couple. All that is necessary to be done is to use the ones cited here as a basis, and by slightly changing the position of the body or of the leg, a different position is obtained with different effects.

In Chapter II you will find the original positions in each of the five methods of fucking, so the following are but variations of these. Each of the following positions is given in a clear concise manner, and the enjoyment of the lovers and their movements are left to the reader's imagination.

163

Ordinary Reversed

The man lies on his back. The woman straddles over him on her knees facing his head, and settles down guiding the prick a short distance in her cunt. She then lays down at full length on the man, chest to chest. The man throws his legs over her thighs and both go to work.

The Trot

The man lies on his back and the woman straddles over him as in previous position, but after inserting the prick, instead of lying down she remains upright, rising up and down on her knees as though on horse back, the man raising his arse in motion with the woman.

The Squat

Similar to the "Trot" excepting that instead of being on her knees, the woman is square over the man on her feet, her knees being up against her bubbies.

Back View

Similar to the "Trot" only instead of facing the man's head the woman faces his feet on her knees. This position enables the woman to press and dangle the man's balls during the action.

The Elastic Cunt

Similar to the "Back View" with the exception that once the connection is made the woman must lean forward over the man's legs, her head over his feet, supporting herself on her hands. The man has a fine view of his manly tool moving in and out of the cunt which conforms to this position as though it were made of some elastic substance.

Cock-Horse

The man lies on his back on a fairly high narron bench, the woman straddling him, and inserting the prick. The woman's legs should be dangling in the air on each side of the bench. The man moves his ass up and down while the woman wiggles from side to side.

Cock-Horse Reversed

Same as above, only the woman faces the other way towards his feet. This position enables her to dangle the man's balls which gives added pleasure to both.

The Bull's Eye

The woman sits on the edge of a table, leaning backwards on her hands. The man gets between her legs and grasping each by the ankle raises them up, bending the legs backwards until

the woman's bull's eye is seen to perfection into
which the man inserts his prick, still holding her
legs in position until the shooting is ended.

Winnowing on the Stomach

The woman lies on her stomach on the table,
her arse and legs over the edge. The man gets
between her legs, and tucking one under each
arm, inserts his prick from underneath her cunt.
He then shoves sturdily up and down, raising his
partner's wiggling ass in the air at each thrust.

Winnowing on the Back

Similar to the above, only in this position the
woman should lay on her back. The man then
has a fine view of his sweetheart's bubbies and
hairy crack during the winnowing process.

Lazy Style

The woman lies on her left side in bed facing
the man, who lies on his right side facing her
and close up against her. The man raises his
hips, and the woman pushes her left leg under
him, so that he is resting on it with his waist on
the right side. She then throws her right leg
over his left hip. This brings her cunt against
his prick and he inserts the tool in its proper
place. They can now fuck side by side. All is
pleasure without any weight to support.

Original Dog Fashion

The woman gets on her hands and knees in the bed, and the man kneels behind her arse. He then inserts his prick in this position. After a short distance of it is in place, he leans over the woman, who should squat down, being careful, however, to keep her bum in the air. She can then reach one hand backward and dangle the man's balls.

Dog Fashion Standing

The woman is on her feet, leaning over and holding on to the back of a convenient chair. The man stands behind her arse thus prettily exposed and inserts his prick underneath into her cunt in this position.

Dog Fashion Lying

The woman lies on her right side in bed, the man lying on his right side directly behind her so that her bum is warming his belly. He lifts her left leg and inserts his prick into the willing crack from behind, letting the leg fall back in place when connection is complete. His hands can then rummage all over the woman's body, tickling her titties and hairy slit.

The Spiked Chair

The man sits on a chair. The woman straddles over him facing him, and settles down on his prick. When connected, she stretches her legs out behind the chair, and they both move their bottoms in unison.

The Spiked Chair Reversed

Same as the previous position, with the exception that the woman straddles over the man the other way, her arse coming against his stomach. When connected the woman leans forward supported by the man's arm, and stretches out her legs, behind the chair.

The Nailed Woman

Same position as for the "Spiked Chair" but when the man's prick is in its warm nook he must place his arms under the woman's knees from the inside and lift them up, placing his hands on her hips. The woman is thus nailed to the man by his prick.

"T" Upside Down

The man sits up in bed, his legs stretched out full length in front of him. The woman straddles over his thighs, and inserts his dagger into her cunt, stretching out her legs to full length behind the man. They then embrace each other, shoving their asses back and forth. This position resembles a capital "T" upside down, from which it derives its name.

"T" Lying Down

The woman lies on her back in bed, her knees up. The man lies crossways underneath her upraised knees, on his right side his prick at her cunt, and her knees over his left hip. Their bodies are now at right angles to each other, resembling a Capital "T" lying down.

The Crossed Scissors

The couple take same position as for "T" lying down. When the connection is complete, the woman places her right leg which is over the man's hip in the previous position, between his legs, leaving her left leg over his left hip. Their legs are now crossed like two pairs of scissors. This is one of the easiest and most comfortable ways of fucking and is such that the prick can be buried to the balls at each thrust without trouble.

The Sharpshooter

The man lies on the bed with his right knee uplifted and the other leg stretched out straight. The woman mounts him crossways putting her right knee on the bed, placing her folded leg underneath his uplifted, and passing her left leg and thigh above the man's left thigh, her foot pointing to the edge of the bed. This brings her

169

cunt above the man's prick half dog fashion and she settles down upon it. The woman is now in the position of a sharpshooter resting on one knee with the other uplifted.

The Toad

The woman lies on her back on the bed, her legs bent upwards and her knees touching her bubbies, with her heels on her ass, taking as little space as possible. A large pillow should be under her if possible. The man kneels at her feet and inserts his prick in her hairy crack, and then bends over, resting his chest on her bended legs.

Reversed "69"

Chapter II gives the original position of French fucking or "69". To reverse it, it is only necessary for the man to lie on his back, the woman straddling over him with her cunt on his mouth, facing his feet. She then pops his upright dagger into her mouth while he plunges his tongue into her cunt.

Lazy "69"

The couple lie full length on the bed side by side, but facing each other, the man's head at her thighs and the woman's head at his thighs.

The man lifts up the woman's uppermost thigh and inserts his head between them, placing his mouth on her cunt, while she does the same to him, putting his prick in her mouth. All is pleasure without any weight to support in this position.

The Setting Hen

The man lies at full length on his back in bed. The woman straddles over his face, facing him, and settels her cunt down on his face, resting on her knees. He sucks her at ease, while the woman reaches behind her and artfully frigs the man's upright prick.

The Real Suck

The man sits on the edge of the bed or on a chair. The woman kneels between his legs and taking his prick in her mouth voluptuously sucks it, tickling and pressing his balls at the same time, until after a few warnng jumps the sperm bursts into her willing mouth. The woman should not cease her sweet love play until all the man's sperm has been drawn from his balls, and his prick begins to get limp. There are many variations of this position. The man can take almost any position, as long as the woman can reach his prick with her mouth. Many men prefer to straddle over the woman as they claim they can secure a better evacuation of sperm when the head of the prick is pointing downward and many women prefer this way on account of the fact that the stuff is spurted with greater force down their throats.

The Selfish Woman

The woman sits on the edge of the bed. The man sits on the floor between her legs, his legs being extended at full length under the bed. Taking her legs, he puts one over each shoulder. This brings her cunt on the level with his mouth and he proceeds to suck her in great style, supporting her arse with his hands. Some women prefer to lie at full length instead of sitting up during this exercise.

Bagpiping

The man sits on the edge of the bed or chair and the woman kneels between his legs putting his upright prick between her two bubbies which she presses tightly around the stiff dagger. The man shoves his arse up and down while the woman moulds her breasts as though she were playing a bagpipe, until the hot sperm bursts from the man's prick hitting her chin and falling back upon her snowy pillows.

The Ride in the Valley

The woman lies on her back on a narrow bench. The man straddles over her, facing her and places his prick between her breasts which he presses tightly around it. He then fucks her bravely in this position.

The Spring

This is the same as the previous position with the exception that the man faces towards the woman's feet. At the critical moment, his stuff escapes from between the two snowy hills and runs down her belly to her hairy forest like a spring, from which this position derives its name.

Armpit Fucking

The woman is seated on a camp-stool or on a chair sideways. The man stands either in front or behind her and inserts his prick under her arm close up to her shoulder. The woman presses her arm to her side and the man shoves sturdily back and forth, until his stuff bathes either the front or back of his partner. If the man is standing behind the woman, she can wet a finger and tickle the rosy head of the prick when it appears at each thrust between her arm and body.

Imitation Bottom Fucking

The man sits well forward on the bed or chair.

The woman backs up to him, leaning forward, which brings her arse out prominently against his prick, dog fashion. The man lays his dagger in the crack of her ass, with its head pointing up her back. He then presses the two ass cheeeks tightly around the prick so as to make the furrow as narrow as possible, and proceeds to shove up and down in the groove thus formed until his sperm bursts up her back, falling down upon her ass.

Every one of the above thirty-two fucking positions is able to be varied in several ways, and the true fucking couple will endeavor to modify each position in every possible manner. However the result is the same, and the warning throbbing of the man's prick, and the gasping of the woman's cunt, followed by panting groans and stiffened bodies precede the final heavenly outburst of seminal fluids on each side, after which the couple rest awhile in each other's embrace to enjoy to the full the delicious feeling of langour which follows each vigorous shooting.

CHAPTER VIII

How to Get the Most Out of Fucking.—Fucking Hints and Secrets.—How to Get a Boy or a Girl.

There are many men and women who keep on fucking all their lives in the one, old fashioned way, and never realize they are not getting all that is possible out of the sexual act. There are also many other couples who have carefully gone into sexual matters very deeply with the result that they have developed the act of coupulation to a high state of perfection. However, these secrets are not common knowledge, there being up to now no book or pamphlet containing them, and those who did know them were apt to keep the knowledge to themselves.

In the first place no couple should slight any one of the five methods described in Chapter II. They should also use all the variations in Chapter VII, and invent more based on these.

Fucking should be done regularly. Every night is not too much for the ordinary married couple provided they make use of the principal of delayed spending or shooting described later.

Each fuck should be at least of one half hour's duration, and should be extended, if possible, to an hour or two hours continual connection. If a couple should fuck in the ordinary way continuing their movements without stopping until the seminal outburst, the length of the fuck would be about two minutes, and would leave them unsatisfied. This provokes them to repeat the operation again and again, which they do without even experiencing the pleasure obtained by one continual fuck of the same duration.

A popular method of shooting is for the man to continue his movements after the first spending until it provokes a second discharge, without removing his prick from the woman's cunt. To those who practice withdrawing, the same effect can be obtained by the woman frigging the man after the first discharge, receiving the second one in her hand. Another popular way is for the woman to suck the man after the first discharge receiving the second in her mouth.

The most pleasure is experienced in fucking if the couple lie in such a position as to enable the woman to massage the man's balls during the action, and especially at the moment of shooting.

176

This forces all the sperm from his balls and re-
sults in a large and plentiful discharge. The man
can also rub the woman's clitoris while fucking
her, which makes her shoot rapidly and frequently, while he is delaying his spending.

Sexual power and desire is increased by the
eating of highly spiced foods, the reading of voluptuous books and looking at erotic pictures. Ten
to fifteen drops of Cantharides (which is a liquid
purchaseable at any drug store) will act quickly
on the sexual organs exciting them and causing
a desire to fuck. Men often put this drug in
women's tea or other liquid unbeknown to them,
which makes the ladies hot, and renders their
fucking a comparatively easy matter. Bathing
the prick and cunt with cold water frequently will
increase the circulation of blood in these parts and
intensify power. Sucking in the French fucking
method also strengthens the organs.

The sexual parts of man and woman are frequently shaved clean of all hair, especially where
sucking is frequently indulged in. In any event
the hair should be kept clipped very short. Previous to sucking, the parts should be thoroughly
washed (a solution of plain borax and water being
good) and the organs and adjacent body bathed

in perfumed toilet water. This adds to the pleasure of sucking.

A large stiff prick is a thing of joy. To increase its size is an easy matter. Frequent sucking will make it larger, and to lengthen it, the prick should be rolled between the palms of the hands as though trying to stretch it out. The ideal method is for the woman to suck the head while she rolls the rest of it between her hands as explained.

The electric fuck is a good strength giver. A small medical battery should be used, the woman holding one handle and the man the other during intercourse, or one handle can be pressed against the man's ass and the other against the woman's, and allowed to remain there without touching. This produces a thousand delicious ticklings inside the cunt which are impossible to get in any other way.

A cock massage is a good tonic for the man. He can lay on his back in bed and the woman gives his cock and balls a good massage, gently squeezing his balls in her hand while frigging him with the other hand. These motions should be gentle at first and then harder and harder until the discharge of his stuff, the woman is shaking the man's prick with a furious motion while pressing his balls with strong firm grasps, kneeding them with her fingers. This should be done to the man once a week, and acts as both a strengthener to his prick and balls, and also as a tonic on his entire body.

The secret of prolonging a fuck is simple. At the first signs of shooting on the man's part, the couple should stop all movements arfd lie perfectly still, the man putting his thoughts on some other subject. After the danger is past they can begin again, repeating this stopping at each threatened outburst. This is called "delayed spending" and is the principal secret of getting the most out of fucking, for by its use the man can prolong the fuck allowing the woman to spend in the mean-time as much as she is able.

"Avoided-spending" is the term applied to the practice of fucking without the man shooting at all. This is done principally by men with vigor-ous partners who like to fuck time and time again in quick succession. By not shooting at all the man is able to accomodate the woman, as each time he inserts his prick in her cunt is the same as a new fuck to her. This method is also in great favor with ordinary couples as a novelty, and is often done when they have a few moments to themselves, it being an easy mattter for the woman to lift her dresses and receive the stiff dagger for a minute or so knowing that the action can be discontinued at will.

"Interrupted-spending" is done by the woman grasping the man's prick firmly at the base right where the canal comes from the balls into the prick. She presses her fingers firmly around the canal just as the man is about to spurt. This keeps the stuff in the man's balls, although his prick throbs and jumps as though he were actually spending.

"All night fucking" is a very common and frequent occurrence between married couples and others, and is largely in use by professional women fuckers. The couple should get in the position of the "Crossed Scissors" described in Chapter VII, after anointing the man's prick with a good supply of cold cream. They can then fuck as usual, using the "delayed shooting" principle described above. They should rest frequently and snatch a few moments of sleep between each "go". This can be kept up all night, the man shooting just previous to getting up in the morning. The benefit lies in the exchange of bodily electricity through the medium of the connection, and the delicious exhausted feeling that follows this long activity is the readjustment of the different organs to the vast amount of energy they have just received. The longer fucking is continued, the greater the languid feeling, and the greater the benefit.

Some women get wetter than others during the sexual act, and the wetter their cunts become the more benefit is derived from the fuck to both. Some women's vitality is such that before the conclusion of fucking, their partners prick is fairly sopping with their stuff which covers his balls and runs down bother their legs. This stuff, being absorbed by the man's prick, is what benefits him in the act.

Many men at times have so much stuff in their balls that it appears difficult for them to get an erection. To overcome this the woman should frig him a few moments before intercourse, which will result in his prick becoming stiff and hard as usual. The theory of this is simple. The stuff descends to the balls, to be discharged through the prick. More stuff is being continually generated, and unless that already in the balls be not drawn off there is no place for it to go except to be absorbed back into the body. When this latter is the case, it throws the man's entire system out of order until the absorption gets in good working order. Consequently a man should either fuck regularly or not at all, for each change from regular fucking to abstinance is a shock to the man's system. Therefore, monks and men not able to be in localities with women have a highly organized absorbing system which relieves their balls from the superflous sperm, while men who fuck have a highly organized discharging system which gets rid of the stuff in the way nature provides it should. It is the changing from one to the other of these systems that is harmful.

How to Fuck to Get Either Boy or Girl Babies at Will.

Many prominent doctors, who have given serious study to this question, have found that boy babies are generated on the right side of the womb and girl babies on the left. The couple who wish to fuck to get, say a boy, must lay in the position of "LAZY STYLE" described in Chapter VII. with the woman lying on her right side. When the man shoots he should press tightly against the woman, burying his prick in her as far as possible and hold it there, the woman, if possible, massaging his balls. This will insure a tremendous outburst of sperm which, owing to the woman's position, will fall on the right side of the woman's womb. The couple should not break the connection after the man has shot until his prick becomes soft in her and it is well to even then keep connected for five minutes longer, at least, so that every drop of his precious liquid is absorbed by the woman. A girl is conceived in just the same way, only the woman should lie on her left side so that the stuff will fall on that side of her womb. After the man pulls out his prick, if the woman then proceeds to suck him, receiving the second discharge in her mouth and swallowing it, the baby's complexion will be clear and white when it is born. The couple should be careful not to fuck in any other position than the one they started with all during the first month. When the woman passes her first period without her monthlies showing up and knows that she is caught, other positions can be used. The woman should remember that the more she swallows the man's stuff the clearer will be the skin of her child. The man's stuff is also substituted for oil or lard by spurting it on the woman's stomach. This renders the skin soft and enables it to stretch during the development of the stomach.

In conclusion, let us remember the word of the famous poet who said:

[You may have good fortune; you may have good luck; But you'll never have anything as good as a fuck.]

183

The Golden Member

T may be useful for you gentlemen to read of the genital strengthening treatment which the doctors subjected me to.

To begin with, I was allowed almost no alcohol, benedictine or sherry I was allowed just before a love joust with my dear Alice, she drinking a similar amount. Raw eggs I was encouraged to swallow as often as possible, I always had three on arising in the morning, flavors with a little sherry.

My bowels were kept regular with extreme care and every day I bathed the genitals with cold water into which a little Florida water had been sprinkled.| My foreskin is a trifle long and I was encouraged to keep the head of my penis covered with it, so that the rubbing of my underclothing would not first irritate and then toughten the head.

The idea being to keep it sensitive for the

185

greater pleasure in copulation. But the penis must be kept scrupulously clean and borax was occasionally used in the water to keep the skin soft and tender like that of a baby.

I was allowed to smoke moderately; exercise, but never on horseback, my mind was kept on sexual matters by means of literature, pictures and sensual music.

This then, was my life for five years and to avoid monotony I was encouraged occasionally to enchant Nora and Berenice—not to mention Corrine, with my carefully developed charms.

Nora, had surrendered to me her maidenhead on the night of my arrival at the Brayson mansion, on the outskirts of an English village.

She loved me passionately, despite her purity of soul, in fact, with her the receiving of my penis into her vagina was a sacred ceremony, to be done only with intense emotion and exaltation.

The throes of pleasure into which I invariably threw her were religious in their nature and it was obvious that the act to her, was neither wrong or immoral.

Berenice was more openly lascivious, her greatest joy was to get my cock into her mouth but this my physician positively forbade except on rare occasions. While such a method did me no particular harm, they say it stimulated the nerves to such an extent that constant practice of it would cause erection and consequent practice became a habit so seductive that it might lead to the exclusion of copulation.

Sucking the cock then, according to them, was not in itself any more injurious than was the emission in the womb, or manual manipulation by another—but self-manipulation or masturbation I was warned was fatal to body and mind alike, since the act itself was nerve wearing to an excessive degree, the waste not only being compensated for by the electricity and magnetism of another body, but its frequency, the habit being once formed, was destructive.

I have spoken of Corinne the tidy young cook, who first admitted me into her lady's boudoir. She was not among the nude nymphs that greeted me and practiced on me the night of my initiation and when I remembered to ask Alice about it, she told me that the reason was: Corinne was deflowered willingly enough by one of my young domestics, but so violently and brutally had he performed on her, that she revolted and swears that there is nothing in copulation for her, and she will never in her present state of mind, give in again.

And, she continued, as long as Corinne attends to her regular duties, I do not care if she is of that mind, and she does you know, sometimes perform on me. I challenge you to overcome her to pleasure and re-seduce her.

So as this young woman was pretty as well as neat, and had a pratically fine outline of hip and posterior and a peculiar grace in walking, indicative of serpentine power, I was nothing loth, but found that I could make but little headway.

The girl would laugh and jest with me, but would not permit me to touch her, even refusing to shake hands.

The case seemed hopeless enough until I hit upon a plan that I confided to Alice. Corrinne was a country lass and had never been in London, so I had Alice send her to the metropolis to do some special shopping, which would require several days.

She did not know it but the same train that took her to London also carried me to the city. Once arrived, Corinne was bewildered, not knowing which way to turn. I watched her without being seen and when a policeman on being appealed to, recommended her to a hotel and secured a hansom for her, I followed to the same hotel.

That afternoon Mistress Corinne assayed to do
her shopping but so ill at ease was she that it
was slow work among the crowd of the great city.
This went on for two days and hardly a beginning
was made in her shopping and I could see that
the poor girl was desperately lonesome, as she
did not know a single soul in London and you
know to be alone in a great strange multitude,
is the quintessence of loneliness.

So I noted, I presented myself at her apartments on the evening of the second day and she
was hysterically glad to see me, merely because
mine was a familiar face.

I suggested the theatre and she gladly welcomed the diversion. When again in the carriage
after the performance, I hinted at supper and she
again agreed. The driver at my directions drove
us to my apartments that I had previously engaged, fitted up. and in a dainty little dining room
we found a table set for two.

The only other person in the apartment was a
discreet waiter. The supper was a success and
so was the champagne—under the influence of the
latter, Corinne thawed out so that I was able to
take her hand without objection on her part. Here
indeed was progress—but the simple act seemed
to arouse her.

189

It is late and we must be going home! she said:
the last course had been served long before but
I had talked against the time and it was now
after two o'clock in the morning. I affected to
be as much surprised as she was and rang the
bell—no waiter—I looked out—no carriage—we
were in a strange part of London far from the
hotel, what could we do?

I will sleep on the floor, dressed, and you can
use the bed.

But do you think that I will allow that, no! I
said, we can share the bed.

Well, I will, if you will promise not to lay a
finger on me while we are in bed—and I do not
need to undress.

But you will be so much more comfortable, you
had best remove your outer clothes and corsets.

Corinne was, I must confess, somewhat under
the influence of wine she had taken and I found
that she was having difficulty in unlacing her corsets, so I came to the rescue and before she knew
it, I had her in my arms, passionately kissing her
arms, shoulders and neck.

Why, you promised, she said, as she broke away,
flushing.

Silently I began to undress, proceeding slowly;
she had made believe to close her eyes but I knew

190

that she was peeping, so I affected to at first keep my genitals covered but in yawning suddenly, being in my shirt and drawers, I raised high my arms and they separated, raising the curtain so to speak of a tremendously erect and palpitating cock.

Then leaving the light burning, I jumped into bed, being careful not to disarrange the bed clothing. I laid flat on my side of the virtuous chair.

There I lay for some minutes, at length I felt a small foot touch my naked leg. I cast a swift look at my bedfellow and caught her peeping at me. Carelessly I threw an arm over and above her pillow, soon after a similar movement on her part brought her naked arm across mine. Her foot advanced up my leg to my knee, her hand gently squeezed my triceps, then crept down my shoulder and body until its progress was impeded by the weight of the chair.

Don't you find the chair in the way of your comfort? I asked, and her reply was a tremulous little sigh. You may remove it and I will trust you to keep your word.

On this I removed the chair and getting back into bed, I managed to lie a little closer to her and managed though it was hard to make no advances.

Again her hand began to explore down my stomach, my thighs, and finally it convulsively grasped what it had all along pined for.

It was terribly difficult but I managed to lie still, although her curling fingers about my cock were thrilling me from head to toe. A moment more and she threw herself upon me, crying out that I would kill her with desire and not try to stop her sufferings.

Upon this I acted, kicking off the bedclothes, I exposed her in only a short chemise. I had on not a stitch of clothes and she did not protest but clung to my cock. To return the compliment, I felt for her vagina, while she complacently opened her legs to assist me.

At the first tickle of my fingers on her love temple, she gave a great heave of her posteriors. It was a perfect and complete surrender.

DELECTUS BOOKS

"The world's premiere publisher of classic erotica." *Bizarre.*

A GUIDE TO THE CORRECTION OF YOUNG GENTLEMEN
By A Lady
The ultimate guide to Victorian domestic discipline, lost since all previously known copies were destroyed by court order nearly seventy years ago.

"Her careful arrangement of subordinate clauses is truly masterful." *The Daily Telegraph.* "I rate this book as near biblical in stature" *The Naughty Victorian.* "The lady guides us through the corporal stages with uncommon relish and an experienced eye to detail...An absolute gem of a book." *Zeitgeist.* "An exhaustive guide to female domination." *Divinity.* "Essential reading for the modern enthusiast with taste." *Skin Two.*
> Delectus 1994 hbk with a superb cover by Sardax 140p with over 30 illustrations. £19.95

THE ROMANCE OF CHASTISEMENT; OR, REVELATIONS OF SCHOOL AND BEDROOM
By An Expert
The Romance is filled with saucy tales comprising headmistresses taking a birch to the bare backsides of schoolgirls, women whipping each other, men spanking women, an aunt whipping her nephew and further painful pleasures.

Delectus have produced a complete facsimile of the rare 1888 edition of this renowned and elegant collection of verse, prose and anecdotes on the subject of the Victorian gentleman's favourite vice: Flagellation!

"One of the all time flagellation classics." *The Literary Review*, "In an entirely different class...A chronicle of punishment, pain and pleasure." *Time Out.* "A classic of Victorian vice." *Forum*, "A very intense volume...a potent, single-minded ode to flagellation." *Divinity*, "A delightful book of awesome contemporary significance...the book is beautifully written." *Daily Telegraph.* "Stylishly reproduced and lovingly illuminated with elegant graphics and pictures...written in a style which is charming, archaic and packed with fine detail." *The Redeemer.*
> Delectus 1993 hbk 160p. £19.95

THE PETTICOAT DOMINANT OR, WOMAN'S REVENGE

An insolent aristocratic youth, Charles, makes an unwelcome, though not initially discouraged pass at his voluptuous tutoress Laura. In disgust at this transgression she sends Charles to stay with her cousin Diane d'Erebe, in a large country house inhabited by a coterie of governesses. They put him through a strict regime of corrective training, involving urolagnia, and enforced feminisation dressing him in corsets and petticoats to rectify his unruly character. Written under a pseudonym by London lawyer Stanislas De Rhodes, and first published in 1898 by Leonard Smithers' "Erotica Biblion Society", Delectus have reset the original into a new edition.

"Frantic...breathless...spicy...restating the publisher's place at the top of the erotic heap." *Divinity*. "A great classic of fetish erotica...A marvellous period piece." *Bizarre*.
        Delectus 1994 hbk 120p. £19.95

PAINFUL PLEASURES

A fascinating miscellany of relentless spankomania comprising letters, short stories. Originally published in New York 1931, Delectus have produced a complete facsimile complemented by the beautiful line illustrations vividly depicting punishment scenes from the book.

Both genders end up with smarting backsides in such stories as "The Adventures of Miss Flossie Evans," and, probably the best spanking story ever written, "Discipline at Parame" in which a stern and uncompromising disciplinarian brings her two cousins Elsie and Peter to meek and prompt obedience. An earlier section contains eight genuine letters and an essay discussing the various merits of discipline and corporal punishment.

The writing is of the highest quality putting many of the current mass market publishers to shame, and Delectus into a class of its own.

"An extraordinary collection...as fresh and appealing now as in its days of shady celebrity...especially brilliant...another masterpiece...a collectors treasure." *Paddles*. "An American S&M classic". *The Bookseller*, "Sophisticated...handsomely printed... classy illustrations...beautifully bound." *Desire*. "For anyone who delights in the roguish elegance of Victorian erotica...this book is highly recommended." *Lust Magazine*. "A cracking good read." *Mayfair*.
        Delectus 1995 hbk in imperial purple d/j 272p. £19.95.

THE MISTRESS & THE SLAVE

A Parisian gentleman of position & wealth begins a romantic liaison with a poor but voluptuous young woman and falls wholly under her spell. The perversity of her nature, with its absolute domination over him, eventually culminates in a tragic ending.

"But, my child, you don't seem to understand what a Mistress is. For instance: your child your favourite daughter, might be dying and I should send you to the Bastille to get me a twopenny trinket. You would go, you would obey! Do you understand?" - "Yes!" he murmured, so pale and troubled that he could scarcely breathe. "And you will do everything I wish?" - "Everything, darling Mistress! Everything! I swear it to you!"
Delectus 1995 hbk in d/j 160p. £19.95

MODERN SLAVES
Claire Willows

From the same publishers as *Painful Pleasures* and *The Strap Returns*, this superb novel, from 1931, relates the story of young Laura who is sent from New York to stay with her uncle in England. However, through a supposed case of mistaken identity, she finds herself handed over to a mysterious woman, who had engineered the situation to suit her own ends. She is whisked away to an all female house of correction, Mrs. Wharton's Training School, in darkest Thurso in the far north of Scotland. Here she undergoes a strict daily regime under the stern tutelage of various strict disciplinarians, before being sold to Lady Manville as a maid and slave. There she joins two other girls and a page boy, William, all of whom Lady Manville disciplines with a unique and whole hearted fervour.

Delectus have produced a beautiful facsimile reproduction of the original Gargoyle edition from the golden decade of American erotica, including 10 superb art-deco style line drawings explicitly depicting scenes from the novel.
Delectus 1995 hbk in imperial purple d/j 288p. £19.95

FREDERIQUE: THE STORY OF A YOUTH TRANSFORMED INTO A YOUNG WOMAN
Don Brennus Alera

A young orphan is left in the charge of his widowed aristocratic aunt, Baroness Saint-Genest. This elegant and wealthy lady teaches Frederique poise & manners and, with eager help from her maid, Rose, transforms him into a young woman, while at the same time keeping him as her personal slave and sissy maid using discipline to ensure complete obedience. Originally published by The Select Bibliotheque, Paris in 1921, this marvellous transvestite tale has been translated into florid English for the first time by Valerie Orpen. The story of Frederique's subjugation and feminisation is accompanied by 14 charming and unique illustrations, reproduced from the original French edition.

Delectus 1995 hbk in d/j 160p. £19.95

MEMOIRS OF A DOMINATRICE
Jean Claqueret & Liane Laure

An elegant and aristocratic Governess recalls her life and the experiences with the young men in her charge. Translated from the French by Clair Auclair from the French edition first published The Collection des Orties Blanches, in Paris, during the 1920s. Illustrated with reproductions of the 10 Jim Black drawings from the original French edition.

Delectus 1995 hbk 140p. £19.95

THE STRAP RETURNS: NEW NOTES ON FLAGELLATION

A superb and attractive facsimile reproduction of an anthology from 1933, originally issued in New York by the same publishers of two other Delectus titles, *Painful Pleasures* and *Modern Slaves*.

This remarkable book contains letters, authentic episodes and short stories including "A Governess Lectures on the Art of Spanking", "A Woman's Revenge" & "The Price of a Silk Handkerchief or, How a Guilty Valet was Rewarded", along with decorations and six full page line drawings by Vladimir Alexandre Karenin.

Delectus 1995 hbk 220p. £19.95

MASOCHISM IN AMERICA OR, MEMOIRS OF A VICTIM OF FEMINISM
Pierre Mac Orlan

A French erotic classic, first published in the 1920s, by surrealist, war hero, and renowned popular thriller writer, Pierre Mac Orlan, this crafted collection of erotic vignettes provides a male masochistic odyssey through America.

Translated, for the first time into English by Alexis Lykiard, and including the five illustrations from the French original.

Delectus 1995 hbk 200p. £19.95

THE SEDUCING CARDINAL'S AMOURS
& THE AMATORY ADVENTURES OF TILLY TOUCHITT
Two erotic classics bound in one volume, originally published by Edward
Avery, one of the most active of the late Victorian erotic publishers.
The first concerns the conquests of a debauched Jesuit Cardinal as he
seduces his way across Northern Italy in the renaissance and is illustrated
with six explicit and rare engravings by Frederillo. The second book
comprises a long letter of confession from a young woman who could
not wait until marriage to loose her maidenhead!
> Delectus 1996 hbk 180p. £19.95

WHITE WOMEN SLAVES
Don Brennus Alera
Set in America's deep south in the years just preceding the American
Civil War this book follows the life of Englishman, Lord Ascot, and his
associates in the State of Louisiana. Originally published by The Select
Bibliotheque in 1910 and written by the prolific author of another
Delectus title, *Frederique*, this book contains all eight original
illustrations.
> Delectus 1996 hbk 270p. £19.95

PAGEANT OF LUST
Peter Linden
Another classic of American erotica from the 1940s in which the erotic
encounters are so frequent and so relentless that the book has an almost
delirious quality that only sensual abandonment can bring. The book is
produced in facsimile along with the eight Francis Bacon style plates by
Raymond Milne.
> Delectus 1996 hbk 200p. £19.95

COMING SOON IN HARDBACK:

Happy Tears, Frida (the sequel to Frederique), Lustful Lucy,
Sacher-Masoch's Venus & Adonis, With Rod & Bum, Earl Lavender,
The Amorous Widow, Maidenhead Stories, Gynecocracy
& many more.

DELECTUS PAPERBACKS

120 DAYS OF SODOM - ADAPTED FOR THE STAGE BY NICK HEDGES FROM THE NOVEL BY THE MARQUIS DE SADE

Four libertines take a group of young adults and four old whores to a deserted castle, there they engage in a four month marathon of cruelty, debasement, and debauchery. The award winning play now available from Delectus, featuring stills from the London production and a revealing interview with the director.

"A bizarre pantomime of depravity that makes the Kama Sutra read like a guide to personal hygiene." *What's On*. "If you missed the play, you definitely need to get the book." *Rouge*. "Unforgettable...their most talked about publication so far." *Risque*.
Delectus 1991 pbk 112p. £6.95

THERE'S A WHIP IN MY VALISE
Greta X

Launching the new Delectus paperback series, bringing you the best erotica from the 50s & 60s, is this superb novel first published in 1961.

A businessman picks up two Swedish hikers and discovers a taste for unusual sex. He is soon searching Europe for the perfect dominant Mistress, and discovers the voluptuous Marlene. Together with her beautiful assistant, who has and acute rubber fetish and decided lesbian leanings, Marlene travels europe to satisfy the strange desires of masochistic men. The plot reaches its climax when five sadistic women, including Marlene and her assistant, descend on the home of Mr. Petersen to give him the time of his life.
Delectus 1995 pbk 200p. £9.99

COMING SOON IN PAPERBACK:

Scream, My Darling Scream, The Whipping Club,
The Libertine, Whipsdom and many more.

EROTICA, SEXOLOGY & CURIOSA - THE CATALOGUE
"For the true connoisseur, there is no better source." *Bizarre*

Delectus are the only global specialists in selling quality antiquarian, rare, and second hand erotica by mail order. Our unique catalogues are dispatched quarterly to almost 5500 customers in over 50 countries worldwide. Prices range from £5.00 to several thousand pounds representing the finest erotic literature from the last three hundred years in English, French, German and Italian including large selections from Olympia, Luxor & Grove Press.

"Mouthwatering lists for serious collectors...decidedly decadent." *Risque*, "The leading source for hard to find erotica" *Screw*. "I have never seen a catalogue so complete and so detailed. A must" *Secret Magazine*. "One of the largest ranges of old and new erotic literature I have ever seen." *Fatal Visions*. For our current catalogue send: £2.50/$5.00

Payment accepted by cheque, cash, postal order, Visa, Mastercard, J.C.B. and Switch. Send to:

Delectus Books, Dept. WS
27 Old Gloucester Street
London WC1N 3XX, England.
Tel: 0181.963.0979.
Fax: 0181.963.0502.
Mail order business only.
Trade enquiries welcome.

(NOTE: Postage is extra at £1.30 per book U.K., £2.20 EEC & Europe, £5.00 U.S.A., £6.00 Elsewhere)

Further publications due in the next few months see our full catalogue for further details.

COMING SOON:
DELECTUS VAMPIRE CLASSICS. A new series featuring some of the best Vampire tales ever written, many for the first time in English.

"Certain publishing houses have consistently merited exceptional praise and recommendations for their offerings. Delectus Books is one such."
Paddles.